SHE LOOKED THROUGH THE SECURITY HOLE but couldn't see the man's face.

"Who is it?" she asked.

"Mac sent me," came the muffled reply.

Erica opened the door.

He stood very still, merging so well with the fog and darkness that for a moment she thought he was gone. Then he straightened his shoulders, as if throwing off a great weight, and stepped inside, into the light.

Dear God—Conner. "No," she whispered. Nothing in her life had prepared her for this. "No, he wouldn't do this to me."

"Yes, he would, and he damn well did—to both of us."

WHAT ARE *LOVESWEPT* ROMANCES?

They are stories of true romance and touching emotion. We believe those two very important ingredients are constants in our highly sensual and very believable stories in the LOVE-SWEPT line. Our goal is to give you, the reader, stories of consistently high quality that may sometimes make you laugh, sometimes make you cry, but are always fresh and creative and contain many delightful surprises within their pages.

Most romance fans read an enormous number of books. Those they truly love, they keep. Others may be traded with friends and soon forgotten. We hope that each LOVESWEPT romance will be a treasure—a "keeper." We will always try to publish

LOVE STORIES YOU'LL NEVER FORGET BY AUTHORS YOU'LL ALWAYS REMEMBER

The Editors

Loveswept ® 810

Mac's Angels:
SURRENDER
THE SHADOW

SANDRA
CHASTAIN

BANTAM BOOKS
NEW YORK · TORONTO · LONDON · SYDNEY · AUCKLAND

MAC'S ANGELS: SURRENDER THE SHADOW
A Bantam Book / November 1996

ISBN 0-553-44550-2

Published simultaneously in the United States and Canada

Bantam Books are published by Bantam Books, a division of Bantam Dou-
bleday Dell Publishing Group, Inc. Its trademark, consisting of the words
"Bantam Books" and the portrayal of a rooster, is Registered in U.S. Patent
and Trademark Office and in other countries. Marca Registrada. Bantam
Books, 1540 Broadway, New York, New York 10036.

PRINTED IN THE UNITED STATES OF AMERICA
OPM   0 9 8 7 6 5 4 3 2 1

My thanks to the following wonderful people who helped me plan this book:

Darian McFarland, AVTECH Executive Flight Center, Atlanta

The folks at the New Orleans chamber of commerce, the zoning office, and the French market

Ann Doggett, who lives on top of Lookout Mountain

Joanne Amort historian Oak Alley Plantation, Vacherie, Louisiana

Rexanne Becnel, romance writer and resident of New Orleans

Ted Hicks, who actually was a Fulbright scholar in Berlin and supplied the background information; my husband, Pepper, who knows more about World War II than most folks who served in it

And last, but certainly not least, to my critique group who kept telling me I could get it all together and make it work:

Ann Howard White, Lyn Ellis, and Patricia Keelyn.

Dear Reader:

When Loveswept decided to devote a month to MEN OF POWER I let my mind drift back to those men who were larger than life, beginning with the superheros I grew up with. At the risk of dating myself, I'll confess that I (as a very young child, of course) was around before television. Radio was my love. At night I would lie down on the floor in front of the big radio in our living room and listen to the adventures of Superman, The Thin Man, Green Hornet, and my favorite, The Shadow.

The Shadow was known primarily as a wealthy man-about-town, a world traveler. But he was more. In his secret life he had the unique ability to slip in and out of places without being seen, thus earning himself the name: The Shadow. He sought to destroy evil, to defend and protect the weak. The more I thought about The Shadow, the more I was certain that I had found the inspiration for my hero. Thus, Conner Preston, my man of power, was born.

SURRENDER THE SHADOW was a real challenge for it is a departure from the kind of romance I usually write. You don't have to lie on the floor in the dark as I did, but I hope you'll fall in love with my Shadow as he rights an old wrong and protects the only woman he ever loved.

Sandra Chastain

PROLOGUE

Lincoln MacAllister studied the file he was holding—Conner Preston. In the ten years since Conner had left Shangrila, Mac had opened it far too often. Conner had never turned him down.

But Mac wasn't certain he ought to use it now. Though the world knew Conner Preston as a sophisticated millionaire importer and exporter, Mac knew the truth, or he thought he had. This time he was worried.

Conner, firmly convinced that he was supposed to have died ten years ago, had become more and more daring, tempting death with a vengeance that skated on the thin edge of self-destruction.

But Conner Preston was the only man on the angel assignment board who could find out what was happening.

Mac picked up the phone and dialed the man adored by the very wealthy and those in need, and feared by the criminal minds of the world—the man known to them only as Shadow.

Halfway around the world, Conner Preston loosened his tie, unbuttoned his shirt collar, and leaned back in his executive chair as he listened to his speakerphone. "You know I'll do anything you ask me to do, Mac, but undercover work for the government is one thing I left behind long ago."

"This isn't for the government, Conner. This is for the ambassador."

"Close enough. When you and I designed Paradox, Inc., we set it up to serve the private sector, remember? If you can afford it, I'll find it, rescue it, or move it—in my own way."

"I remember and I wouldn't ask if it weren't important, not just to the ambassador but to others. Shadow is the only one who can stop this disaster."

Conner swung his chair around so that he could look out the window of his Venice apartment and see the slow-moving water in the canal beyond. Ten years ago he'd promised to repay Mac for saving his life and helping him find a use for the skills he'd learned as a Green Beret.

His buddies had given him the nickname Shadow because he could get in and out of dangerous places without being seen. Conner Preston had been the best at what he did and he'd thought it would never end.

But he'd made one mistake. He'd fallen in love with Erica Fallon. He'd been on top of the world when he and his brother Bart had gone to the little chapel on what was to have been Conner's wedding day.

But instead of a wedding, Conner had been shot and Bart had been killed.

And the bride had never shown up.

"You don't have to do it alone, Conner," Mac said. "If you refuse, I'll understand. I'll find someone else."

Conner stood and walked out on the balcony, allowing the lazy sound of the boatmen moving gondolas along the water to sooth his anger. "No, you won't, Mac. I'd be dead or in prison if it weren't for you. I owe you and you wouldn't have called unless I were the only one who could pull it off. But I work alone."

"Not this time, Conner. The woman who brought the ambassador here is the key to the mission."

"I see. And who is the woman wielding all this power?"

There was a long pause.

"Erica Fallon."

Long after Conner had broken the connection, Mac sat thinking and tapping the folder on his knee. It was done now, and the wisdom of his decision was no longer in question. He picked up the phone, dialed a number, and waited for it to be answered.

"Erica, he's on his way. It's in your hands now."

ONE

Conner Preston felt a burst of white-hot anger slice down his spine. He welcomed the sensation. It told him he was alive and reminded him that danger was just ahead. This time the danger was a murderer. And he'd been waiting ten years to confront her.

Following Mac's instructions, Conner left his rental car in the parking area at the base of Tennessee's renowned Lookout Mountain and bought a ticket on the famous Incline Railroad. His destination was only a block from the station at the top.

The train was empty. People who lived in the village used the winding, foggy road on the back side of the mountain, and there were no sightseers on the last trip of the day to the battlefield park hidden at the top.

As the train jerked to a start and inched upward, Conner fastened his attention on the wooded area along the tracks. The lighted car made him an open target on the slow, steep climb. He didn't like being exposed. Anyone could be waiting out there and not be seen. His sense of danger heightened.

Finally, the car reached the end of the line. Conner stepped off and watched as several women, maids, he guessed from their conversations, boarded the train for the ride down.

From the observation platform, Conner took one last look at the valley below. A cloud slowly moved between him and the rising sliver of the December moon. It cast an opaque web of black over the twinkling Christmas lights of the sprawling city of Chattanooga and the Blue Ridge Mountains beyond.

Conner buttoned his overcoat and walked out of the empty station into an early evening mist so thick that it muffled the sound of the tram returning to the bottom of the mountain.

Behind him, the lights went out. The darkness was ideal. It fed the smoldering anger that had followed him across the Atlantic to confront the woman responsible for his brother's death.

His fury intensified. The fog swirled around the streetlights, turning their glow into faint smears of luminescence. Exaggerated shadows of trees and buildings reached from the sides of the streets to conceal his presence—perfect for a man who spent most of his life in hiding—a man called Shadow.

As he looked around, streaks of light and dark seemed to lift, then swoop to gather their tattered wisps. He felt as if he stood in some kind of unnatural cold, wet smoke. Taking a quick glance down the murky street, he wondered if Mac could possibly be right. Could she be here, in this strange, surrealistic community perched in the clouds?

Erica needed help and Mac had sent Conner. If Mac's request was intended to soften Conner's hatred toward her, it hadn't. He had listened when Mac said it was time he faced the truth about the past, whatever it was. But Conner wasn't buying any plea to forgive and forget. Wisely, Mac hadn't made one. He'd simply asked Conner to come.

What bothered him was why. Mac knew how Conner felt about Erica, the constant anger that fueled his daredevil missions. He'd rescued Peace Corps advisers, nuns, sick and wounded children who needed medical attention, but this ambassador was a nobody, a state department official without a post. If the world learned he'd been shot, they probably wouldn't even recognize his name.

How Erica had come to be his administrative assistant, Conner couldn't imagine. She'd been an artist when they met, determined to make her mark on the world. Erica was like a whirlwind that had scooped up a brash young soldier and carried him to places he'd never dreamed of. In her own way she'd been as much a risk-taker as he.

Now Mac had taken the wounded ambassador to safety at the Shangrila medical compound and asked Conner to protect Erica. For his own reasons as much as Mac's, Conner agreed.

Only Mac knew what had happened ten years

ago in Berlin, though Conner was no longer sure either of them knew everything.

The German newspapers had reported the murder of Bart Preston, the bright young American architectural student attending the Technical University of Berlin. Little mention was made of the other American, a soldier, who was badly wounded. It was considered just another assault on the military by some left-wing group seeking publicity to support their claim that outsiders were behind the move to tear down the Berlin Wall.

Only a few insiders knew that the two victims were brothers, or that the site of the attack was a little historic church whose minister had been engaged to perform a wedding. And the press didn't know there was a third American who was missing from the scene—Erica Fallon—Conner's future bride.

Erica was supposed to meet Conner and Bart at the church. Instead, it was two masked gunmen who'd tied up the minister, ransacked the chapel, and waited inside. Afterward, Bart was dead. Conner, with gunshots in both legs, was stabilized and flown to a military hospital in the states. The army would handle the investigation. The army would find Erica and tell her what happened. The army would keep Conner informed.

According to Mac, it wasn't until later that the military investigator learned the reason for Erica's absence—a change of heart about the wedding and an early morning flight to Paris.

In a few moments Conner had lost his brother, the woman he loved, his military career, and for a time, his will to live. But Mac had stepped in and refused to let him quit. Mac recognized the potential for Conner's unique experience and convinced him that he could use his military skills to set up his own business.

Conner never heard from Erica. Mac said she'd stayed in Paris. By the time he was ready to leave Shangrila, Paradox, Inc. was a reality and he had realized that there was no room in his life for a permanent personal relationship. He'd sworn he'd never see Erica Fallon again. He didn't dare. He hoped instead that life would be her punishment, as it was his.

Conner Preston operated his import-export business with sophistication and flair. But his undercover services, for those who could afford them, were carried out by a man known only as Shadow.

For ten years Conner searched quietly for the mastermind behind Bart's assassination. At the same time he rescued or found lost people, places, and objects—everything from the ordinary to the bizarre, from the legal to the not so legal. He'd been incredibly successful because he had nothing to lose. His life had ended in the chapel, watching his brother die. Now he belonged to Mac and those who needed him most.

This time it was personal. Conner's official objective was to protect Erica. Shadow's mission was to finally confront the woman he would forever hold responsible for Bart's death and expose the evil in her heart.

If Erica Fallon had ever had a heart.

As the wind pushed against the back of the house, Erica heard every sound, every creak of the walls, every brush of a branch against a window. She was running out of time and she didn't know what to do.

Mac had been willing to take the ambassador, even with the risks involved. He'd even offered Erica sanctuary, but she knew the truth—the bullet Ambassador Collins had taken was a warning to her.

Ten years ago Erica had learned about warnings, to believe them or unconscionably bad things happened. Once again she was being deliberately drawn into something evil and she had no idea what the evil was.

Or why.

And who was Mac sending to help her? Why had he been so mysterious, referring to him only as "the man"? She folded her arms across her chest and squeezed. The house was warm. It was her heart that was cold.

It had been that way for a very long time.

When the doorbell rang, she jumped. Her throat closed off and she couldn't swallow. He was here. It had to be Mac's angel. No one else knew where to find her. At least she didn't think she'd been followed. And, except for the ambassador, she'd kept her connection to her family home in Tennessee a secret.

Erica stepped into the foyer, glanced into the mirror, then chastised herself. What difference did it make how she looked if she was going to die?

The streetlight beyond the security hole kept her from seeing the man's face.

"Who is it?" she asked.

"Mac sent me," came the muffled reply.

Erica opened the door and stepped back to let the man inside.

He stood very still, merging so well with the fog and darkness that for a moment she thought he was gone. Then he straightened his shoulders, as if throwing off a great weight, and stepped closer, into the light.

Dear God—Conner. "No," she whispered as she caught her throat with her fingertips. Nothing in her life had prepared her for this. "No, he wouldn't do this to me."

"Yes, he would, and he damn well did—to both of us."

Conner Preston took a cold close-up look at the woman he'd once loved. Loved, then hated, then dismissed.

At least that was what he'd thought. He'd been wrong. Just looking at her brought it all crashing back.

She'd changed. Ten years ago she'd been so young and determined, so full of life, convinced that the world was hers for the taking. And she had taken it as though there were no tomorrow.

Her live-for-the-moment philosophy had seemed curiously at odds with her reason for being in Germany. She'd been an art history student on a Fulbright scholarship studying the design of historic buildings. That was how he'd met her, through his brother Bart, who was an architectural student in the same program.

As Americans, Bart and Erica had been partners and friends. Then Conner had been transferred to Berlin and reunited with his younger brother.

From the moment Conner had laid eyes on Erica, he'd been completely captivated. For weeks, he was the third member of their team. They'd minutely measured, photographed, and studied the little chapel that was the focus of their project. Conner hadn't understood his brother's love for the old church, but he'd dissect the Empire State Building if it would keep him close to Erica.

They'd measured and sketched the historic structure for hours, even crawling through the ancient catacomb of tunnels. Once, when a crawl space came to an end, Bart managed to find a trigger mechanism that got them beyond the false wall. He'd been ecstatic to find a broken piece of marble that he was sure came from an ancient sculpture. He'd sworn Conner and Erica to secrecy to protect his discovery from treasure hunters.

Then Erica did something she'd never done before. She left the work to Bart while she and Conner shared private picnics at Tiergarten Park and Wannsee Lake, visited coffee houses, where they drank strong espresso and ate the local specialty, hot dogs and French fries with mayonnaise. Erica fell in love with as much determination as she approached her studies. And the studies were left behind in the wake of newly discovered passion.

Erica was the most exotic woman Conner had ever met. She'd heard his buddies call him Shadow and demanded a special name of her own. Because of her flair for the dramatic, he'd laughingly called her his Dragon Lady. Her midnight-black hair had been long and straight, falling across her shoulders to the middle of her back. The first time they'd made love she'd teased him by covering her breasts with it.

Conner closed his eyes, trying to shut out that memory. He couldn't. It slammed into him with sonic force.

A gust of wind blew dry leaves across the porch in a rustle, reminding him that they were standing in the light. Out of habit, he glanced behind him.

Erica stepped back and in a tight voice said, "I guess you'd better come in, Conner."

"Yes." He found it oddly difficult to speak. The ease of their past relationship was long gone and the new emotion between them was dangerously volatile.

He shrugged out of his overcoat while Erica closed and locked the door.

The click sounded like a shell falling into the

chamber of a gun. Conner patted his jacket, instinctively reassuring himself that his own weapon was within reach.

"You won't need that here," Erica said as she took his coat, careful that their hands didn't touch. "At least I don't think you will. But then, I'm not sure of anything anymore."

Once, the catch in her voice would have moved him. Then he remembered what she'd done. "Whatever you know is more than I know. Talk to me, Dragon Lady."

He used his secret name for her mockingly.

"Would you like some coffee?" She turned toward the kitchen as if she had to escape from the bitterness he made no attempt to disguise.

Conner followed her without comment, focusing on the house to give himself time to regroup.

Except for the appliances, the kitchen was straight out of the forties with glass-windowed white cabinets full of neatly stacked dinnerware. Erica went into the pantry and brought out two mugs that she set on a small table nestled in the three-sided bay window overlooking the valley below.

While she filled the coffeemaker with water, Conner walked over to the window. He instinctively hugged the edge of the wall and looked out. The elements had thrown a cloak of opaque gray over the house, closing them inside. He didn't need to worry about being visible. He couldn't see beyond the blank panes of glass.

Soon the sound of grinding filled the silence, and the rich smell of coffee beans permeated the air.

Finally, Erica spoke. "First I want to say I'm sorry, Conner—about what happened to you—and Bart. I—"

"You damned well ought to be. He died because of you."

He heard her gasp and saw her face pale in the reflection of the windowpane.

"I couldn't have changed anything. By the time I knew, it was too late. All I can say now is that I'm truly sorry."

"If you'd told me you weren't going through with the wedding, neither of us would have been there. Or was it a setup all the way? I've often wondered about that."

"You think I knew what was going to happen? No, don't answer that. I can see that you do. You actually believe that I arranged to have the man I loved more than life itself wounded and his brother killed." She spoke rapidly, then paused and took a deep breath. "Your brother was my partner, my best friend."

"You disappeared without any explanation. I call a person who does that a coward."

Conner didn't say murderer, but he could have. And she knew that was what he was thinking.

"I know you don't believe this, Conner, but I had no choice. And then—then it was too late. Staying away from you was safer."

He had to hand it to her. She almost sounded

sincere. If he turned around and looked at her, he was certain he'd see those big black eyes swimming in tears held back through sheer willpower. There was a time she would have cried. She was tougher now.

"Forget the explanations, Erica. I wouldn't believe you anyway. Whatever the reason, you left me standing at the altar. Bart got caught in the crossfire. And you were responsible."

"Then why did you come? Obviously Mac told you I'd be here. I can't understand why he didn't extend the same courtesy to me."

"Believe me, I wouldn't be here—except for Mac. Suppose you tell me why he thinks you need help." Conner turned slowly to face her, daring her to refuse.

She blanched, catching the counter as if she might have fallen otherwise.

"He asked me to protect you, Erica. I agreed. That means I have a job to do and I intend to see it through, even if I would rather cut and run."

"Do you have to be so cold, Conner? Can't you give me even the smallest benefit of the doubt?"

"Not in this lifetime, lady. The last thing I want to do is rehash what might have been. There was a time when I wanted to know why. Not tonight."

But Erica wasn't going to let him get away with using mental force. "All right, Conner. I admit I should have explained."

"Why didn't you?"

"I tried, but I couldn't find you. Then later I

understood that it was better if I let you go. What about you? You knew where I was. I sent word that I'd wait for you in Paris. You never came. In one afternoon I lost everything too."

Conner felt his gut clench. She almost had him believing her, until he remembered Bart. And if she'd sent a message, Mac would have told him. It was time to end the discussion. He didn't intend to let this turn into a scene of bitter recriminations. The quicker he got to the bottom of her problem, the quicker he could get back to the life he'd built for himself.

"You'll excuse me if I can't rouse a lot of sympathy for your pain, if you felt any. In fact, I'd like to deal with the present."

Conner's words said one thing, but his pulse was pounding and his mouth was dry. He couldn't look away without giving her a hint of his faltering control. So he watched her with a narrowed gaze. She was dressed in coveralls made of shimmering spandex that fit like skin.

A voice inside him whispered, "Get the hell out of here, Conner. She's trouble and you're about to get caught up in it again."

"I'm waiting," he said. "What kind of danger are you in?"

"Not yet, Conner, we have to talk about what happened in Berlin. I think it's connected to this new trouble."

"Tell me about this new trouble and I'll decide."

"*You'll* decide? I think you'd better know, Conner Preston, that *you* don't make the decisions." She took in a deep breath. "I'm sorry, but you're here to help me, not give orders."

God, she was beautiful. He could see her agitation and he felt a startling response in his own body. Help her? That was the last thing he had on his mind.

Now he understood that old reference to the thin line between love and hate. In spite of what she'd done, all he wanted was to find the nearest bed and plunge into her, ravish her like some old-world invader taking claim to a land he'd fought for. Hell, he didn't even need a bed.

Then she raised thick-lashed eyelids and gave him a look that said she knew exactly what he was feeling.

Conner forced his reply. "That's yet to be decided—whether or not I will help you." He might as well make her squirm. "Just so we understand each other, what's in it for me?"

There was no point in trying to protect him any longer. "You misunderstand, Conner. I never expected Mac to send you. I wish he hadn't. You see there's another person in danger. Shadow. I assume that's you, unless someone else has adopted that persona."

"What does Shadow have to do with this?"

"The person who shot the ambassador said if he didn't get the book, next time he wouldn't miss."

"What book?"

"If I knew that, I wouldn't need you, Conner.

Something else very odd happened. I got a call from the ambassador's office this morning. It seems we're about to receive a belated wedding gift."

Conner grabbed her wrist and pulled her so close that he could feel her breath on his chin. "What do you mean, wedding gift?"

"A package from Berlin arrived at the ambassador's old office in Paris. They are forwarding it here. It was addressed to Lieutenant and Mrs. Conner Preston."

At that moment there was a shatter of glass and Conner heard a whistle. He slammed Erica to the floor and fell on top of her.

"What are you doing?" she asked, struggling to get out from under his protective cover.

"Shut up, Erica, and stay down."

"Why?"

"Somebody just took a shot at us."

TWO

Conner listened intently. All he could hear was the coffee dripping into the pot. "How many entrances are there to the house?"

"The front, the kitchen door that goes into the garage, and the door from the study to the deck."

"Are they locked?"

Erica thought for a moment. "I'm not sure about the study door, but the rest are."

"Other than Mac, who knows where you are?"

"Only the ambassador. I never give this address out."

"Who lives here when you're away?"

"My aunt, but she goes to Florida every winter. What about you? Could you have been followed?"

"No," he snapped, then thought about it. That tickle of awareness shimmied down his spine, the same kind of awareness he'd felt on his trip up the mountain. He'd been pretty steamed when he left the Chattanooga airport and headed for the Incline Railroad. Maybe somebody had been behind him. He couldn't be sure.

Then again, maybe the feeling came from the woman beneath him and not someone outside.

"So," Erica said in a tight whisper, "what do we do now?"

Conner stared down at her. They were almost nose to nose. In fact, noses were about the only parts of their bodies not touching. He felt her breasts press against him as she breathed. She still wore that light floral fragrance that triggered the memory of picnics and wildflowers. His lower body responded to that scent, making it imperative for him to move.

"Stay put." Conner gritted his teeth and wondered what moment of lunacy had made him think that he could see Erica and not want her. Even with a shooter outside the window he was more aware of her sensuality than her safety. He couldn't protect her by lying there. And he was placing himself in another kind of danger—the danger of remembering.

Abruptly he rolled away, crawled swiftly to the wall where the light switch was located, reached up, and flicked it off.

"Conner, wait. I'm coming with you."

But, like a ghost, he was gone. With her heart hammering in her throat, Erica inched her way past the breakfast bar and into the corridor, where she could see both the front door and the study at the other end. At that moment an errant shaft of moon-light slipped through the fog and beamed like a spotlight to the deck. As far as she could tell, that door hadn't been opened.

Agonizing minutes passed. Where was he? God, she hadn't wanted him there. But she could not ignore the instant awakening of desire within her.

Suddenly a figure appeared in the moonlight. The glass door opened and a man cautiously slipped inside.

"I don't know who you are," Erica said, "but I have a gun and if you take one step closer, you're going to regret it."

"I regret it already," Conner said. "I thought I told you to stay put in the kitchen."

Erica tried to swallow her sigh of relief. "And I told you that you aren't giving the orders around here."

She sat up, folded her arms around her knees, and tried to control the bout of trembling that swept over her. When the ambassador had been shot, she'd been concerned about him. But this was different, more personal somehow. Or maybe her collapse was tied in to Conner's presence.

"I think he's gone, Erica, but I can't be sure. We need to get out of here."

But she couldn't move. Her limbs had turned to mush, along with her brains. "My knees and I have decided that we'll just sit here for a minute," she said in a voice that was raspy and strained. "Besides, unless you have wings, we can't go anywhere before morning."

Then Conner was reaching for her, lifting her into the warmth of his embrace, and for a moment she just leaned against him, allowing his strength to restore hers.

"Don't you have a car?"

"No, I don't keep one here. I took a taxi from the airport. I stay off the Scenic Highway during the winter. I'll call a cab."

For a minute Conner continued to hold her, then, realizing what he was doing, released her and stepped away. "All right, but keep your voice down."

Erica stumbled, caught the wall, and felt her way back to the kitchen and the wall phone by the door.

"The phone is dead," she whispered.

"Dead phone and no car. I don't like this. We're sitting ducks up here and it's hunting season."

"Do you think he's going to kill us?"

"I don't know. Maybe he's just playing with us."

"Conner, why? I don't understand."

"Neither do I—yet. Right now we need to get to a safe room, a room with only one door and windows he can't get to. Is there a basement?"

"No, this mountain is almost solid rock. What about the attic?"

"Too secure. He'd have us cornered there. No, it needs to be a room we can get out of if we have to."

"There's a small office off the study," she suggested. "It has only one door. The windows overlook the valley and there's an adjacent bathroom."

"Fine. Can you find your way around in the dark?"

"This was my home, Conner. Of course I can."

"I'll check out the house while you get the coffee and some food. Then," he said in a voice so impersonal that Erica shivered, "I want information."

She stared at him blankly, then nodded. For just a moment he'd held her, but it had meant nothing. She felt colder now than she had on the floor. The man she was seeing was Shadow, the Green Beret, not Conner.

She had to show him that she was calm, even if it wasn't true. Pulling herself together, she walked past the broken glass on the floor to the refrigerator, where she braved another shot by defiantly opening the door to take out cheese and grapes. When she turned, Conner was gone. Next, she stepped into the tiny pantry, closed the door, and flicked on the light long enough to find a box of crackers.

Two trips to the office moved the food, coffee, and the makings for more. She concentrated on her task, delaying any thought of the coming confrontation with Conner.

Without sound or movement, Conner suddenly materialized in the small room. "I brought blankets for us to sleep on." He dropped the blankets, closed and locked the door.

"Help me," he said in a deep whisper.

"Help you what?"

"Move this chest in front of the door."

"You seriously believe that whoever fired that shot is coming after us?"

"Would you rather wait and find out?"

Erica fought the sudden nausea that swept over her and leaned against the heavy antique chest, moving it slowly toward the door. Suddenly they were sealed inside the room. Choosing the office was a mistake. It was too small. Conner seemed even bigger than he had before. He sucked up the air and filled the space.

"Pour the coffee," he said sharply. She wondered if he too might be fighting the unexpected pull from the past.

In the dark, Erica opened the crackers and cheese, arranging them along with the fruit on the small coffee table before a tiny fireplace. She poured coffee into the mugs and set out the cream and sugar.

"It's ready."

After a moment he turned and walked toward her, no longer hugging the shadows.

"I'll light the fire," she said, and moved away, fighting the sudden tremor that racked her body.

"No. A smoking chimney will tell him where we are."

"There'll be no smoke. The logs aren't real."

"Then why light it?"

"Because . . ." she whispered between teeth that chattered in spite of her effort to keep them still, "I need to feel warm."

As she turned on the electric logs, she heard the creak of the floor as Conner sat down and leaned against the couch. He bit into a cracker and chewed slowly, the sound a ticking reminder of what was to come.

"Now, start at the beginning and tell me what's happened, Erica."

There was a lump the size of a rock in her throat. She couldn't have spoken if she'd wanted. To delay her answer until she had full control, she dropped to the floor at the end of the table and reached for her mug. She started to add sugar, then stopped. Right now she needed the strong bitter liquid to keep her focused.

"First . . ." she began softly, then jutted her chin and spoke more firmly, "I can understand why you don't want to talk about the past, Conner, but I have to explain what happened."

"Your explanation comes about ten years too late, don't you think?"

He wasn't going to make it easy, but she didn't deserve it to be easy. "I know you don't want to hear this, but I had no choice. I would never have done anything to hurt you—or Bart."

Conner laughed. "Seems to me if that was your goal, you'd have bought three tickets to Paris instead of one."

She felt as if he'd punched her in the stomach. "Tickets to Paris?"

"I'm just curious. How'd you manage it, Erica? Getting out of West Berlin? Was it really a last-minute attack of cold feet, or did you and your lover already have your tickets?"

"Conner, I swear to you, I didn't go to Paris, at least not then. And the only lover I had was you."

His hand shot out and clasped her wrist tightly. "Don't lie to me, Erica. I went to the church expecting to meet you and Bart. Bart arrived—alone. Why weren't you with him?"

She jerked her hand away. She couldn't talk to him if he was touching her. "Because he came by my room the night before, looking for you. When he found out you were gone, he said something about picking up our wedding gift. He said he'd meet us at the church."

"There were two people who did meet us at the church, uninvited guests for our wedding, Erica—assassins. Bart was killed and I might as well have been. Where were you?"

"I don't know. They took me away—someplace dark and cold."

"They? You want to explain that? Somehow it doesn't make a lot of sense—none of it. The night before you were so sure. As I recall, you wanted to wake the minister and have him marry us then." Conner tightened his grip on her arm. "You could have told me you'd changed your mind. Instead, you let us go to that church. Why?"

The flame from the artificial logs gave off just enough light for her to see his face. There was something about the tormented look in his eyes that said he believed she'd stood him up intentionally, that she hadn't wanted to marry him. She swallowed, taking in the hard lines of his face and knew again what she'd lost.

Conner Preston had been the kind of man who walked into a room and captured the imagination of every woman there. He didn't need the green beret to draw women. He didn't have to smile at them. In fact, he rarely did, but they recognized his power. Blond and blue-eyed, he filled the custom-fitted dress green uniform to perfection. Conner Preston was the physical prototype of the American soldier. But more than that, he'd been brash and daring, with the kind of magnetism that reached out and touched a woman, branding the innermost part of her. One intimate gesture, one brush of that power, and she'd felt like the most important woman in the world. She would never deliberately have hurt him.

"If I hadn't been so crazy in love with you, I'd never have followed their instructions."

"Their instructions? Whose instructions?"

"They came just as I was about to leave. They said that you'd sent them to bring me to the church. It never occurred to me that they were lying."

"They? You keep saying they. Who were these mysterious messengers, Erica?"

"I don't know. All I knew then was that they were wearing the uniforms of your unit. By the time

I figured out that they weren't Green Berets, they'd kidnapped me."

Conner let out a disbelieving laugh. "Members of the Special Forces kidnapped you? But they let you go, didn't they? Doesn't that seem a bit odd?"

He was mocking her, but in truth, he knew that could have happened. As a Green Beret, a man was trained for covert operations. He followed orders without question. Kidnapping a woman would have been a simple mission.

"They drugged me, kept me for two days."

"What did they want you to do?"

"Give them the notes on my art project and then leave Berlin."

"Notes? You mean all those sketches of buildings you and Bart made? Why?"

"I don't know. I didn't argue. I thought we'd broken some kind of law. I gave them my sketchbooks and Bart's portfolio. They told me to stay away from you and keep quiet or the next time we'd both be killed. Then they let me go."

"And you took the next plane to Paris. I'm touched by your concern."

The tears that had collected behind her eyelids threatened to spill over. She swallowed hard. "No. I was frantic with worry. I went straight to the base. The military police questioned me for two days before they told me you'd been taken back to the States. They said the best thing I could do was follow the assassins' orders."

"And that was it? You've had ten years to get in touch, Erica. I haven't been hard to find."

"I wrote to you, Conner."

"I didn't get any letters."

"There was only one."

"Only one?"

Any faint hope she might have had to make things right between them died as she heard the derision in his voice. "I was young and scared, Conner. And, silly me, I actually thought you'd come back for me. I waited, but you didn't."

From Conner's expression, Erica knew he didn't believe her. "I understand your anger and I can't change it, but I believe there is some kind of connection between what happened then and the present. Somehow, because of me, Bart was killed and now the ambassador's been shot."

Conner's silence said it all. He was a soldier who still stood for truth, honor, and justice. For now she had to be content to think he was considering her words. She could understand his disbelief; she'd felt the same way over his abandonment. They'd been in love, desperately in love. She'd always consoled herself with the certainty he would never have walked away and left her if he'd known the truth.

And so she'd waited. Then one day she lost the baby he never knew she was carrying and it didn't matter anymore.

Now they sat, staring at each other, no longer touching, yet still connected by the tragedies that had touched their lives.

Erica glanced down at the angry red fingerprints on her wrist. She felt branded. Her skin still tingled, the sensation radiating up her arm.

"Conner, what were you really doing in West Berlin? Could the assassin have thought that Bart and I were working with you?"

"No way, Dragon Lady. I was just part of a team sent in to protect any visiting government officials. There was nobody special in West Germany at the time. It makes no sense. Why is somebody stalking you now?"

He brushed right past the threat to himself.

She rubbed her wrist. "I'm sure you know that in the last seven years, since the Berlin Wall came down, certain artworks missing since World War Two have been sold on the black market."

"I'd heard."

"I assume you know that the treasures in question disappeared during the German invasion of Europe. People have been searching for them ever since. It was rumored that they were hidden under the German headquarters in Berlin. Some said they were beneath a lake, in an underground cavern, even divided up among the officers, who sold them to buy a new beginning after the war."

"I know. Finding art and antiquities are my business, but what does any of that have to do with you and the ambassador? Talk to me, Erica. I'm listening."

"The ambassador is the chairman of a three-man committee appointed by the United Nations to look into the black market sale of missing artworks that belonged to the people of occupied Europe."

Conner just waited.

"Brighton Kilgore is one of the committee members. He told us that he was dealing with a mercenary known as Shadow who was close to learning the identity of the sellers. I knew it had to be you."

Conner concealed his surprise. The only time Brighton Kilgore had contacted Shadow, he'd been turned down.

"I suppose you discussed me with Kilgore?"

"No, of course not. I didn't even have a chance to tell the ambassador. He was shot as we were leaving our first meeting. That's when he told me to call Mr. MacAllister. Ambassador Collins said Mac knew you, that I could trust him to keep me safe."

"What's your part in this?"

"I went to work for Ambassador Collins in Paris, nine years ago. I'm his administrative assistant. Didn't Mac tell you about all this?"

"He told me about the committee. I already knew you worked for Collins."

That statement said it all. He'd known all along where she was, and he'd never made any effort to contact her. Erica's last vestige of hope vanished. So be it. Where Conner had once been tough, now he'd become hard and unyielding. She could be that way too. If she had to work with him, she'd find a way to do it. He'd never find out she still cared for him.

"I don't know what they're after, Conner. I just know they're prepared to kill to get it."

"Tell me again what happened," he said. "All of it. Word for word." Conner leaned forward as if to intimidate her.

It did. "The man with the gun deliberately shot the ambassador. Then he said 'We want the book. If we don't get it, you'll be next.'"

"And you're sure you don't know anything about a book?" Conner asked.

"I have no idea what he was talking about. But obviously he thought I did."

The coffee cooled. The tension heightened. In this one tiny segment of time, nothing had changed. Erica and Conner were together again. She held her breath, afraid to move.

Then she let the air out of her lungs and pulled away. She was doing just what she'd sworn she wouldn't. Emotionally she was still as drawn to Conner as she had been that first night their eyes met across the smoky tavern. They'd once made a commitment to each other that should have included trust. For whatever reason, that trust had been shattered and nothing could bring it back.

At least he was talking to her. "I was hoping," she said, "that you might have learned who shot you ten years ago."

"No, the incident was covered up so completely that even the army has no records. The only thing we can figure is that it had something to do with the political situation in West Berlin at that time."

"Conner, I know this is painful for you, but why did they shoot Bart? There was nothing political about him. He was such an innocent, such a gentle soul."

"He was just talking to them and reached in his pocket. I think they thought he had a gun. The sons of—they killed him. The second man shot me too, once in each leg. Then they panicked and they ran."

"Bart had a gun?"

"Of course not. I didn't know what he was going for until later."

"What was it, Conner?"

Conner gave a short laugh, placed his mug on the table, and stood. "Our marriage license."

THREE

Conner walked to the window overlooking the valley. The fog had blown away while they were talking. Now he could see the lights of Chattanooga below. It was hard to believe it was Christmas. Without family or close friends, Conner paid the holiday little mind, pausing only to curse the shutdown of commerce between December 25th and New Year's Day.

"You don't have a tree," he said.

"You mean a Christmas tree?"

"Yes. You used to be sentimental. I remember the Easter bunny you put on my pillow."

Sentimental? Others might argue with that. Conner was the only one who'd ever seen the vulnerable side of her. Just when Erica thought she'd drawn the perimeters inside which she could effectively operate, Conner erased them. How dare he talk about what they'd shared when he'd taken it away so callously? Those memories were private, something to keep hidden away, to treasure.

"You used to have a sense of humor. Where'd it go?"

"I don't know. Death has a way of making you serious." He turned to face her, leaning against the wall beside the window, his arms folded loosely across his chest. "You know we can't do this, don't you?"

"Do what?"

"Work together as if nothing ever happened between us. Something did happen and the hell of it is that it's still there. I didn't expect it and I don't like it. Lust gets in the way of logic."

"Lust?" She swallowed her sense of incredulity and asked, "That's the way you remember it?"

"No, that's the way it is now."

She tried to hide the pain he evoked with his words, then realized that pain—and distance—were what he was going for. "We don't have to work together, Conner. You can walk out that door and keep going."

"No. You and I both know I can't."

Even in the half-dark he was pinning her down with the incredible blue of his eyes. She lowered her gaze and found herself staring at the toes of his shoes. Shoes? She was staring at his shoes when all she wanted to do was look at him.

She skidded away from the end of the table and turned toward the fire, anything to break the connection between them. "Just how do you expect us to get past the lust?"

He noticed that she said us, suggesting that she was still as attracted to him as he was to her. "I've always found that bringing something into the open took away the mystery."

"Fine. How do we do that?"

"I could be wrong, but I think this might be the only way." He walked toward her, holding out his hand, palm up.

She laid her hand in his and let him pull her up and draw her close. With every move her awareness heightened, her sensitive nerve endings reacted. He was giving her time to turn away, to stop what was happening.

She did neither.

Then he flipped her hand behind her and pulled her against him.

For a minute they glared at each other, measuring, daring, neither flinching.

"You always were a witch, Dragon Lady. You haven't changed."

"And you always were so sure of yourself."

"Not this time," he growled, and lowered his head.

The kiss started hot and got hotter. With his lips he was demanding, punishing, taking. She gave him the same in return. He walked her backward, pushing her until her body pressed against the desk and she could go no farther. Then, with one hand he lifted her so that she sat on the edge, and he was between her legs.

His arousal pulsated against her, and she moved to meet it with abandon. Deeper and deeper his tongue delved into her mouth, exploring, sucking. He pulled away, took a long, heated look at her, then recaptured her lips with devastating greed.

Then suddenly he leaned back and started to slide his arm beneath her knees.

"No, don't," she said in a voice taut with emotion. "I'm not going to do this. Kissing leads to making love and that . . . to—no! Let me go, Conner."

"What's wrong? Don't you believe in confronting a problem head-on?"

"Sometimes. But I've been down this road before and I'm not interested in the pain at the end of it." She pushed him away, rubbing the back of her hand against bruised lips. Old memories rushed back. Being pregnant and alone was scary, but nothing was as bad as what had happened next. She'd lost one baby. She'd never hurt like that again.

"Too bad. Sex is a pretty powerful mediator."

"It's also a dangerous substitute for that logic you referred to. We're a lot wiser now, Conner, a lot stronger. There has to be another way."

"I hope to hell you're right."

"Let's start with fresh coffee and we'll—we'll examine what we have."

He looked down at his still prominent erection

and in a flash of the old Conner quipped, "I'd say that what I have is fairly obvious."

Erica hoped he hadn't noticed the marbled tightness of her nipples pressing against the silky fabric of her jump suit. She didn't want to think about the ache she felt in even more private places.

Moments later they'd each claimed opposite corners of the couch and were watching the flames licking at the artificial logs in the fireplace before them. Erica searched for less intimate conversation.

"Tell me about Shadow, Conner. What's he been doing for the past ten years?"

He frowned as if he didn't want to answer, then asked, "Are you familiar with Paradox, Inc.?"

"Yes, I've heard about it. Mac said you import and export fine gifts. You've been very successful. How'd you learn about those things?"

"I didn't. I have developed a kind of photographic memory and I have an assistant, Sterling. Sterling knows everything about every item we sell. She's taken on the task of sophisticating me."

"She?"

Erica couldn't keep the dismay from her voice. Of course Conner had a woman, many of them probably. But being confronted with it in such affectionate tones was hurtful. "She's apparently done a good job. I've heard that Conner Preston is the darling of the international set, a real man about the world. But what about Shadow?"

He hesitated for so long that Erica wasn't certain he was going to tell her. Then he put his cup on the table beside the couch and leaned forward, as if he needed the warmth of the fire.

"Let's just say that Mac and I have managed to find a use for Shadow's talents."

"And is he still a member of the Special Forces working undercover?"

"That Shadow is no more, Erica. He died along with my army career. Not much market for unconventional warfare in the civilian world."

"Why don't I believe you?"

"I don't know. Why don't you?"

"Because Mr. Kilgore seemed very sure that you could find the truth. I'm not sure the others were too happy with his hiring you."

"Let's get one thing straight, Erica. I'm not working for Brighton Kilgore. Tell me about the committee. Who else is involved?"

"There's just the ambassador, Mr. Kilgore, and Karl Ernst."

"Karl Ernst? How very interesting. A politician and two thieves."

"Nonsense! Mr. Ernst was chosen for his knowledge of the missing art treasures and his position as a government official in Berlin. The committee was Mr. Kilgore's idea. He was added because as an art patron he's underwriting part of the expense of the committee."

"And the ambassador?"

"As a young man Ambassador Collins was part of the official governing party sent in with the occupation forces to carry out the restructuring of Germany after the war."

"Doesn't the composition of the committee strike you as a little odd?"

"What do you mean?"

"Examine the connections between the past and the present. Brighton Kilgore, present-day entrepreneur, says he's hired Shadow, who once spent time in Berlin. The ambassador, currently an American government official, has you, a former student in Berlin. It makes me wonder about Mr. Ernst's tie to the past."

"Well, there's only one other person I can think of who is connected to the two of us and Mr. Ernst."

Conner's lips narrowed. "Yes. Mac."

She shook her head. "I was thinking of Bart. At the time, Mr. Ernst was Bart's adviser at the university."

Conner swore.

"Does that make a difference?"

"I'm not sure."

"This is awkward for you, Conner. Mac should have sent someone else."

"It isn't something I'm excited about, but it may be a new link to Bart's murderers. And it's pretty clear that we have to see this through—whatever we might want. Mac was right. Nobody else has the answers."

"Answers?" Erica snapped. "We don't have any answers. I don't even understand the questions."

"Neither do I—yet. Help me spread out these blankets, Erica. One of us will sleep while the other keeps watch. I'll take the first shift."

"This is my house, Conner. I'm the one who was shot at—twice. You go to bed and let me think."

He smiled at her, more tenderly than he knew. "You aren't the only one, Dragon Lady. Ten years ago I was shot at. That shooter didn't miss."

After midnight, when Conner was certain that Erica slept, he used the cellular phone in his coat pocket to call Mac. Mac answered instantly. Did the man ever sleep?

"Mac? Conner here. I'm on top of a damned mountain in Tennessee with Erica Fallon. Somebody took a shot at us. You want to tell me what this is all about?"

"I told you all I know. The ambassador was shot and Erica's life was threatened. Are either of you hurt?"

"No. If the shooter had meant to kill the ambassador, he would be dead. I think *someone* wanted to bring Erica and me together again. Would you know anything about that, Mac?"

"No, it's not what you're thinking. Ten years ago the ambassador was kind enough to help answer questions about what happened at the church. When he asked for protection for Erica, I felt obligated to supply it."

"Mac, is he aware you sent Shadow?"

"He believes I sent Conner Preston."

"You know Kilgore is saying that he hired Shadow to search for the treasures."

"Yes. I checked with Sterling, who denied it. Interesting isn't it?"

"But you think this is somehow connected to Berlin and Bart, don't you?"

Mac hesitated for a long time before saying, "Maybe, but I haven't found the link. Any ideas?"

"Not yet. You know Erica says she didn't make it to the church ten years ago because she was kidnapped by Green Berets. Do you know anything about that?"

"No. I was told at the time that the incident was classified. The military claimed she needed money. Her bills were suddenly paid and though they could never prove it, they believed it was her payoff for setting up you and Bart. When she made no effort to reach you, there was no reason to question that conclusion."

"Then how was she able to work for the ambassador? Didn't she have to go through some kind of security clearance?"

There was a long silence. "Conner, she passed. The money was her own. What do you think of her story?"

"I think she's a very convincing woman when she wants to be. Until I find some reason to believe otherwise, I'll take the military's explanation. I'm beginning to think she's right about what is happening now. This is connected to that Sunday at the church."

"Is there anything I can do?"

Conner glanced over at the sleeping figure sprawled across the wine-colored blankets in front of the fire. "Yes, send snow."

"Should I ask what that means, Conner."

"No." There was no way he could tell Mac that Erica's house was a sexual oven and he was being broiled alive.

It was the mountain, he decided, and the fog that came and went, creating the eerie atmosphere around the gray granite structure that was the Fallon family home. He'd paced the room for hours, the thick carpet muffling the sound of his footsteps and leaving nothing but tension behind.

"So what are you going to do?" Mac asked, bringing Conner back to the present.

"I don't know yet. But come morning, we're leaving. Waiting is something I've never been good at. I think it's time for Shadow to meet the players in this little charade."

"Starting with?"

"I'm working on it, Mac. I'll be in touch."

Conner stood at the window looking out. As Shadow, Conner Preston had gone just about anywhere he wanted and accomplished what he set out to do. Trying to make sense out of this situation was like trying to catch smoke.

He was fooling himself. When that bullet shattered the window, just missing Erica, everything changed. He'd spent ten years holding first Erica, then himself responsible for Bart's death. Now Erica was in danger and the hell of it was that he couldn't walk away and let her die no matter what she'd done.

Conner sighed. When Brighton Kilgore had contacted Shadow to look into the sudden appearance of lost World War II art treasures on the black market, he'd turned him down, preferring to investigate on his own. That familiar feeling of danger had drawn him in.

As if some mastermind were orchestrating the event, the players had been pulled together; three from the past and three from the present. Though the ambassador was, from what Conner could deduce, an innocent party, Erica, Ernst, and Kilgore had all turned up on a committee charged with locating the looted treasures. Coincidental? Not likely. But why had Kilgore announced to the committee that he'd hired Shadow?

Conner was deliberately focusing on everyone involved—except Erica. He couldn't avoid that any longer. What was her part in all this? Was she setting him up again?

Conner decided it was time Shadow and Brighton Kilgore had a little talk. The situation might prove a bit tricky since officially there was no connection between Shadow and Conner Preston. Anyone who dealt with Shadow could reach him only through a private number.

Now Conner would have to make personal contact with Kilgore. In the past he'd always made it a practice to avoid any contact with Shadow's clients, prospective or otherwise, but this time he'd have to make an exception. He'd become the sophisticated playboy he was expected to be.

"Something wrong, Conner?"

Conner groaned. "I didn't mean to wake you, Erica."

"It's hard to sleep while you're pacing about like a caged lion. Why didn't you tell me you had a phone?"

He thought about how she'd felt in his arms. "I was distracted."

She let it pass. "Do you think Mac is trying to throw us together?"

So she'd heard his conversation. "Mac isn't that subtle. He'd say so. He just wants to protect you."

"What do you see out there?"

He didn't turn. "Fog. How come I never knew about this place before?"

"It was part of my past, a past I tried very hard to get away from."

"Why would you want to leave? I think I'd like it here," he admitted. "It's like a private world, sheltered from the outside."

"When the snow is two feet deep, it's really sheltered. When my parents were still alive, we called this place home but it was never really ours. We just passed through when my father was between 'opportunities.' There was a time when all I wanted to do was get away from all this history, tradition, and failure. Neither he nor I could ever live up to the family's expectations. I felt smothered here."

"And now?"

"Now I come here when I want to be alone."

"I can't imagine that you were ever considered a failure, Erica."

"Well, I was. Growing up, I was plain and shy."

Conner laughed. "I never saw that Erica."

"I wanted to be an artist but I was told I had no talent. So I studied art history and pretended. I never finished college, never completed my art history project, never had a regular job." She gave a bitter laugh. "Just like my father."

"What happened to him?"

"He and Mother were in a car that drove off an embankment in the mountains of France. The result of another 'adventure' gone wrong."

"But you could come here," he said, almost adding, *why didn't you?*

"Yes. I could come here. That's what my father would have done."

So much for safety. The Erica he knew would never hide. She'd do just what she was doing now, challenge life. "Tell me about the history and tradition," he said.

"The tradition is that sooner or later all the Fallon women come here to live out their lives—alone."

"That's pretty depressing. What about the history?"

"That's easier. Just down the street is the park where the Battle of Lookout Mountain was fought during the War Between the States. They say that sometimes, in the winter when the mist is thick, you can see the soldiers' ghosts."

"I can believe that," he said. "Tonight I felt a shiver or two as I walked down the street."

"As kids, we used to sit on the cannons and wait for the ghosts to appear. All we ever accomplished was scaring ourselves to death."

"That's not so hard to do."

"I find it hard to believe that you are ever scared, Conner."

"Believe it, lady. There are times I'm scared to death. This is one of them."

Conner turned around. From the light of the fire she could see his bare feet. The first article of clothing Conner shed was always his shoes. At some point he'd unfastened his belt and unbuttoned his shirt.

For the last five minutes, through half-closed eyes she'd watched him pace, smiling at the picture of his tousled hair, his bare feet, and wrinkled clothes. No longer the immaculate executive who had appeared at her door, he looked as if he'd just climbed out of bed. There'd been a time when it was their bed he'd just climbed out of and the trousers had been regulation camouflage. She'd loved seeing him in uniform. He'd been dangerous and appealing—just like he was now.

Before he'd walked away from her.

Before he'd blamed her for Bart's death.

Erica sat up and leaned toward the fire, her chin resting on her crossed arms. Absentmindedly she fingered the zipper in her jump suit, gasping when a strand of her hair inadvertently got caught.

Conner stepped forward before he thought. "Let me." He pushed her fingertips away while he tugged at the metal tongue. But the more he moved the fastener down, the farther she had to lean to ease the pain and the closer she came to his bare chest.

By the time he worked the strand of hair free he'd exposed most of her breasts and the sound of his breathing was as uneven as her own.

"Thanks," she said, and scooted away. "I'm sorry I brought you into this, Conner. I honestly wish I could do things over."

"Honesty? Now, there's a commodity in short supply."

"And Shadow?" she snapped. "Does he deal in honesty?"

"Shadow does what he has to do. But you know that, don't you? Why do you think Kilgore told the committee about Shadow? I would have thought he'd keep his nefarious little enterprises to himself."

"I'm not sure. I had the feeling that it was a kind of threat. Either Mr. Ernst would come up with something, or his man would. Mr. Ernst asked who his man was and Kilgore said that he'd hired a mercenary known as Shadow."

"What makes the committee think this isn't just

some kind of hoax? There've been rumors of Hitler's secret vault of treasures for fifty years. But nobody has ever found it."

"The art treasures are not a rumor, Conner. Brighton Kilgore owns one of them."

"He does? Which one?"

"Before World War Two, two identical statues of the Virgin Mary flanked the altar of a small church in France. When the Germans invaded, the statues disappeared. Kilgore has one of them."

That surprised Conner. Why would he say he'd hired Shadow to find the artworks if he already owned one of them?

"How would you feel about spending Christmas in New Orleans, Ms. Fallon?"

"If you're looking for Santa, I think you're a bit too far south."

"I stopped believing in Santa Claus a long time ago. No, we're going to call on my old friend Brighton Kilgore."

"We? Won't he think it odd that you and I are together?"

"Maybe, and maybe not."

"In the meantime, I'll let you keep watch while I grab a few winks. My guess is our shooter is gone, but I've been wrong before."

Erica walked to the window and looked out. Faint patches of light smudged the fog in the eastern sky. "When are we leaving?"

"When does the first train run down the mountain?"

FOUR

Instead of driving to the Chattanooga airport, Conner headed for Atlanta, an hour and a half away. The schedule was better and if the local airport were being watched, their destination would remain secret, at least for a while.

Conner turned in his rental car and bought the last two first class tickets to New Orleans on the next flight.

"I haven't been to New Orleans in years, but I've been told that you can't find rooms without a reservation," Erica said, "certainly not the week before Christmas."

"Not rooms. A suite. And I keep one at the Claridge."

"Why?"

"Because I never know when I'll be in town. I also have an office there."

Erica knew about the Claridge. Housing both

offices and living quarters only the very wealthy could afford, the classic building was located at the edge of the French Quarter, overlooking the river.

Erica began to understand how very successful Conner Preston had become. The brash, swaggering young soldier had been replaced by a sophisticated mercenary in a cashmere suit and Italian shoes. Along with the new facade came the deadly surety that Conner would set the rules of their relationship and she would have no choice but to follow them—if she wanted his help.

And she did. She needed Shadow. She wanted Conner.

Erica watched the Atlanta skyscrapers turn into tiny playing pieces on a gameboard as the airplane moved through the clouds and gained altitude. At least it wouldn't be as cold in New Orleans as it had been in Tennessee.

Cold. As the sun caught the edges of the clouds, they looked like they were brushed with ice. The illusion took her back to the day the ambassador was wounded. Snow had been blowing into their eyes as she and Ambassador Collins had stepped out of New York's Waldorf hotel onto Park Avenue. Christmas shoppers and departing office workers had quickly surrounded them.

When the man in the ski mask appeared beside them, Erica hadn't noticed he had a gun. Not until he'd aimed it at her, then the ambassador, and fired. Only Erica had heard his warning as he leaned against her and then vanished into the crowd. "Give them the book or you'll be next."

The ambassador was an old man and he'd been good to her. It wasn't right that he should suffer because somebody wanted to get her attention.

But it had worked. Now it was up to her not to let that attention wander. Because of that warning, Conner Preston had finally come to her, but it was too late for them. He obviously had no feelings for her—except for his openly declared lust, and they'd put that temptation behind them.

"Does Brighton Kilgore know you're Shadow?" she asked.

"No. He's an art buyer and Conner Preston is in the import-export business. We've crossed paths before both socially and professionally."

Erica continued to look out the window. "I'm confused. Tell me. How do you keep Shadow and Conner separate? How does one go about employing Shadow without working through Conner Preston."

"He calls a private number and reaches an answering machine. He leaves a message. Sterling follows up on the call and works out the details. If she determines the matter is something Shadow should look into, then he makes contact, by phone only."

"And where does one get that number?"

"Only from someone who has contracted with Shadow in the past. But Shadow turns down a hundred assignments for every one he accepts."

Erica turned her attention from the sunlight beyond the window to Conner. She'd scooted to the corner of her seat so that they didn't touch. But it hadn't helped. They were still too close. They may have addressed the question of lust, but its promise was still there.

"And what made you reject Mr. Kilgore as a client?"

"Shadow doesn't deal in illegal activities for personal profit."

"What do you expect to accomplish in New Orleans?"

"You know Kilgore lives in New Orleans. I expect to wrangle an invitation to one of his famous Christmas celebrations at his River Road plantation. I want to see the statue for myself."

"Why is it important that you see it?"

"It isn't. I intend to learn where it came from."

"I see. And how will you explain me?"

"You have it wrong, Dragon Lady. You know Kilgore. You'll explain me."

"And how do I do that?"

He thought about that for a moment. "That's simple, Erica. We were once engaged to be married. I suspect Kilgore knows that. We met again in New York when I attended a party in honor of the new United Nations director of trade. We've since rekindled our relationship."

Erica gasped. She and the ambassador had attended. Brighton Kilgore had attended, but she hadn't seen Conner. "Were you really there?"

"Briefly. I had to leave."

"I didn't see you."

"I know."

But he'd seen her. From a distance, and even that was too close. Through the years he'd managed to avoid all contact with her—until the ambassador was reassigned to the States. Since then it had become more difficult. He always knew where Erica was—but that time somebody had messed up.

When he entered the embassy foyer he'd seen her. Bart was dead and she was alive. Emotion had overwhelmed him so completely that he'd known getting closer was a risk he wasn't ready to take. For a while he'd stared at her, taking in her self-confidence, the new maturity of her beauty. Until she'd laughed and, as if she'd known he was there, turned toward the door.

Conner had stepped quickly behind a bronze statue. For just a moment he'd thought she'd seen him. Then, as if perplexed, she shook her head, laughed gaily, and turned back to the guest. Always the dedicated employee, Erica had moved from one group to the next, charming them with her smile and attention and that way she had of physically touching them.

Just as she'd once done to Bart and later, more intimately, to Conner. She was shy, but she knew how to use her body, how to convey a sense of innocence and charm. Every man there wanted her and was convinced that she had special feelings for them.

Before he could do something that would destroy everything he'd built, Conner had turned and left.

Erica Fallon was a fake and a liar. He'd known that then, and now as he studied her he knew how very good she was. The promise of intimacy was still there, not offered, but implied. He didn't believe for one minute that her pushing him away in the office back in Tennessee was anything more than a ploy to keep him interested.

For now he'd go along with that. For now he'd work with her. But he intended to make her pay for her sins. He'd use the lust she didn't want to acknowledge to make her want him every day for the rest of her life. Like he wanted her.

She thought the past was connected to the present. She didn't know how right she was.

"That was a pretty small bag you brought on board, so I assume you aren't prepared for the kind of socializing I expect us to do." Conner let his seat back and closed his eyes. "Make a list of what you'll need, Erica. It's important that Conner Preston and Erica Fallon take New Orleans by storm."

"I know you're accustomed to acting alone, but I would be less likely to foil your plans if I had some idea of what you have in mind."

"The prime objective is locating the art treasures by finding out who shot the ambassador and threatened you. For this, the prime operatives, Shadow and his Dragon Lady, are undercover. Sorry," he said with a dry laugh, "bad choice of words. But the idea is worth considering."

❖————————❖

The hotel had been designed to blend with the old wrought iron balconies and ornate trim of the buildings in the French Quarter. Inside the atrium, moss green wrought iron rails were draped with garlands sprinkled with twinkling white lights and pink bows to match the hot pink color of the walls. In the center, a fifty-foot tree strung with more white lights and frosted with artificial snow looked very real. Cheerful Christmas carols played softly as the guests moved purposefully along.

Conner quickly checked them in and headed down a private corridor almost hidden from view. He stepped into the glass cubicle and inserted his card. As the small elevator moved smoothly up the side of the atrium, Conner felt that prickle of ice zipper down his spine. He glanced down at the lobby, looking for an explanation. They were being watched.

"Something wrong, Conner?" Erica studied his face, then glanced around the hotel. She was too observant, realizing instantly that he was uneasy. Conner swore silently. It wasn't like him to allow his feelings to show. At least not his true ones.

But the uneasiness was still there and he knew better than to ignore his intuition. He reached out and pulled Erica into his arms. "Smile, darling. It's show time."

Her instinctive resistance was quickly covered by the touch of Conner's lips. She wasn't prepared for the onslaught of feelings his kiss set off. For just a second she responded, then realized what she was doing and began to struggle.

Conner slid his lips to her ear. "Act like we're lovers, dammit. Somebody is watching us."

Erica stopped fighting him and reluctantly allowed him to reestablish the kiss. The pressure of his lips changed, became more gentle, asking.

And that asking changed everything.

When he finally pulled back, he planted a surprisingly chaste kiss on her forehead and let out a deep ragged breath. "First thing you have to learn is to follow directions."

Erica gasped, gave a convincing lurch, and came down on his toe with the heel of her shoe. Between gestures of concern, she gave him her most charming smile and said, "And the first thing you have to learn is to ask, not order!" She cut her eyes back toward the curved walkway around the rooms. "Who's watching us?"

"I don't know."

She moistened her lips and nodded her head. "Uh-huh. Here we are, two people in an elevator, at least two hundred feet away from anybody, and you know we're being watched. How?"

"Instinct. Believe me, I'm never wrong."

A second elevator slid past them going down, an elevator with one occupant—a man with his back turned.

"Is your office a part of your suite? Conner?"

"No. The office is on the third floor."

"How many offices do you have?"

"Paradox, Inc. is headquartered in Virginia, but I have branches like this in Vienna, London, and San Francisco."

Erica jerked her gaze to meet his. "No office in Germany?"

His clipped no and the opening of the elevator door forestalled another question.

She followed him into a foyer, trying to ignore the lingering taste of his mouth on hers, and fighting her growing instinct to run. He used his key to open a door to the right and they stepped inside. The room was exquisite. Her aunt had always said that old money was quiet, and new money was loud. She was wrong. If this suite were any indication, Conner's new money was a mere whisper of elegance.

Erica slipped off her black coat and stood in the middle of the parlor. "Sterling's work?" she asked.

"Not the suite." He locked the door and with one flick of the switch turned on the two lamps on either side of the couch. "But she found the hotel."

"When do I get to meet this paragon of good taste and unique abilities?"

"You don't. Sterling never leaves the Virginia office. That is your bedroom," he said, nodding to a room opening off the parlor. "I have some calls to make, then we'll have dinner."

"I prefer to eat in my room."

"We'll dine in the Bienville Restaurant on top of the building. They serve an eclectic variety of excellent food, but more than that, Brighton Kilgore has a reservation for dinner this evening."

"And how do you know that?"

"Mac." Conner glanced at his watch and started toward a door at the opposite end of the room. "It's six o'clock. I dine at eight every night."

Erica bit back a sharp retort. Better save her disagreements for battles that counted. Besides, she was tired. She'd had little rest the night before. What she needed now was an aspirin and a shower.

Still, she didn't intend to make anything easy for Conner. "*Every* night at eight? How predictably dull. Shadow has certainly changed."

He stopped and turned back to face her. "Believe me, Dragon Lady, there's nothing dull about Shadow. I still enjoy certain pleasures. And now I'm in a position to make sure they're available."

She laughed uneasily. "I would have thought those pleasures came a little later in the evening for a worldly man like you."

"I have developed a weakness for chocolate, especially after midnight."

Erica felt a lurch in her belly. A picture flashed across her mind of dark sweet chocolate drizzled across her nude body. "Everybody knows that eating after midnight isn't good for you."

"I've found that *everybody* isn't always right."

"Really?"

"I make up my own mind and I'm honest about my weaknesses."

She looked at him, unable to stop herself.

"It's true," he whispered. "I told you that honesty is important to me, Erica. I never lie."

She raised her eyebrows in challenge. "There's always a first time."

"Maybe, but this isn't it."

He was telling her she could trust him. Dare she? "How can I be sure?"

"It isn't midnight yet."

Behind her closed door Erica listened for a moment to make certain that Conner wasn't going to follow her. Then she moved toward the cherry desk by the window and picked up the phone.

From memory, she punched in Mac's number and was rewarded by an instant answer.

"Mac, this is Erica. I'm afraid I'm going to have to ask you to call Conner back. This isn't going to work out. I think it would be better if I handled this myself."

"Erica, Conner is your best chance of getting to the bottom of these attempts on your life. I think you ought to put your personal objections aside and work with him."

"How's Ambassador Collins?"

"Still frightened, but improving."

"All right, Mac, I'll go along with Conner—for now. But I wish you'd speak to him about . . . about . . ."

"About what, Erica?"

"Never mind. It wouldn't do any good anyway."

Mac laughed. "Don't I know it?"

Erica hung up the phone, hearing the unmistakable click that told her Conner had been listening. He hadn't heard anything, but his audacity made her angry. Two could play whatever game he was playing.

He wanted New Orleans to take notice of Conner Preston and Erica Fallon. She'd make certain they did. She glanced in the mirror and knew it would take more than a nap to make that happen. She'd buy herself a new dress all right, one that would make Brighton Kilgore sit up and take notice. At the same time, she'd teach Conner not to underestimate her.

Instead of taking a bath and a rest as she'd been told, Erica slipped out of the suite to go shopping.

Conner, hearing the click of the suite door swore and pulled his jacket back on. He waited inside until he heard her get on the elevator. Where was she going? Was she meeting someone? He'd heard only part of her telephone conversation with Mac. Another elevator slid open and he stepped in. His was just above and to the side of hers. She was alone.

In the lobby, Conner hung back to listen and watch as she headed for the concierge desk.

"Where is the nearest dress shop?" she asked.

"We have a lovely boutique right here in the hotel," the woman replied, and directed Erica across the lobby.

Conner was forced to skirt the atrium to remain

hidden, though Erica seemed so intent on her errand that he wasn't sure she would have noticed him following her.

Once inside, Erica browsed through the rack of garments and frowned as she studied the price tags. The store had two entrances that Conner could see; the one into the hotel lobby, and another that led to the street. Conner hid himself by a rack where he could see both doors.

When Erica moved out of view into a dressing room with several dresses over her arm, Conner beckoned to the proprietor. "The lady is my fiancée and we just had a fight. She always shops to punish me. It makes her feel better. I'll pay for what she buys, but if she sees me she's liable to go out the back door. I mean—if there is one. Is there?"

"No, sir."

He relaxed and leaned back against one of the building supports. "Don't tell her I'm here," he said with a wink. "I'm supposed to be surprised."

The proprietor nodded. She wanted to make the sale as much as Conner wanted her to.

The first dress was midnight blue, entirely too short and sassy. As she turned from side to side before the mirror, he could see flashes of lace at the top of her thigh-high hose. *Don't you dare buy that dress, Erica. The last thing I want to do is fight off every man who looks at you.*

She took one last look at the price tag and shook her head. Conner let out a deep breath of relief when she reappeared moments later in a black dress. It covered every inch of her, from her chin to the floor. Until she turned around. The dress had no back. He swallowed hard. Erica had to be wearing the world's smallest bikini, or nothing at all.

"Could you come in here, please?" she called out to the clerk.

Conner almost took a step forward. The woman shook him off. "You're not here," she whispered. "Remember?"

He nodded. "Let her think she's charged it and put it on my tab—Suite 1601."

The clerk nodded and vanished into the room, then returned carrying a red dress across her arm, a dress that Conner never saw modeled. Moments later Erica appeared in her regular clothes, stopped at a rack he couldn't see clearly, then handed something sparkly to the woman ringing up her purchases. Next she riffled through her wallet and pulled out a credit card.

"The only other thing I need is a pair of heels, red. No, silver."

In a loud voice, the proprietor of the shop directed her to a shoe store next door.

Damn, he hadn't counted on that. Now he had to scramble to catch up and still remain hidden.

Erica, arms filled with packages, stepped out onto the sidewalk and was swept up in the throng of office workers, Christmas shoppers, and tourists. He'd almost reached her, when he saw a man step up directly behind her. He gave her a deliberate push, sending the packages in one direction and Erica in the other.

Conner dodged a shopper and came abreast of Erica just as the man melted into the crowd and disappeared. He couldn't leave Erica alone to go after him. Conner swore and knelt beside Erica, who was white-faced and shaken.

"Are you hurt?"

"No, I'm not hurt," she snapped. "What are you doing here?"

"Let's get back inside, darling, and examine your knee," he said, biting back an admonishment for the risk she'd taken. He took her packages in one hand and held her arm tightly with the other, giving her no chance to disagree.

Inside the lobby, he slid his arm around her shoulder and walked her across the atrium.

"How dare you follow me?"

"Erica, may I remind you that your life is in danger? Suppose he'd pushed you into the street?"

"Well, he didn't. As you said, it's obvious he doesn't want me dead. He just wants my attention. He got it." She rubbed her knee.

"Mr. Preston, I saw what happened." The worried doorman had followed them inside. "Is Miss Fallon hurt?"

"I don't think so," Conner answered.

"Shall I send for the house doctor?"

"What about it, darling?"

"No—no, really, I'm fine."

With a show of concern, Conner inclined his

head so that they were almost touching. "If you'd said something, I'd have arranged to have a selection of clothes brought directly to our suite for your approval."

"I wanted to make my own choices," Erica said between barely clenched teeth. She shrugged her shoulders, trying to put some space between them.

Conner held tighter. "Move it, Erica," he growled under his breath. "This isn't the kind of attention I wanted to draw."

For a moment Erica felt the blood drain from her head. She swayed, catching on to his arm automatically, else she would have fallen.

Conner took one look at her face and handed the packages to a hovering bellman. "What's wrong, Erica?"

She could only shake her head.

Conner tightened his grip on her waist and steered her onto the elevator. "Are you sure you weren't hurt?" he asked, concern overriding his arrogance.

She caught the iron rail that circled the elevator as it began to rise. "If you don't let me go, Conner, it won't be the floor of the elevator I'll hit. And I don't care who is watching."

Conner understood her reaction. She was covering her fear with anger. The incident on the sidewalk had to have been more frightening than she'd let on.

Moments later they were back inside the suite.

"How did you plan to get back in here?" Conner asked, holding up the room key. "The elevator won't leave the lobby without the right key."

"Then give me one."

"I don't think so. I see now that I can't trust you."

"Conner," she began wearily, "you may be some kind of superman, but you aren't my lord and master. We're going to have to reach an understanding about that."

"What did he say to you, Erica?" he asked abruptly, changing the subject.

"Just like before. He says he wants the book. He said he could get to me anywhere."

"Damn! Did you recognize him?"

"No. I don't even know if he was the same one who shot at the ambassador. That man was wearing a ski mask and his voice was muffled."

She headed toward her bedroom. The earlier need for an aspirin had reached gigantic proportions. "You can forget about going to dinner."

"Why? Unless I miss my guess, this box contains a dress."

"Yes, but I was going to buy a pair of shoes, when I was torpedoed."

"You don't have another pair?"

"Not to match my dress."

"What kind of shoes do you need?"

She rubbed her knee and gave a disbelieving laugh. "What else? Silver slippers. High-heeled silver slippers."

FIVE

"Are you sure we have to do this?" Erica asked as she followed the maître d' to a choice table in the center of the restaurant.

Conner's hand felt like a hot iron at the small of her back. That combined with the stare of every eye in the place made her want to disappear into the thick carpet beneath her feet. Conner had wanted them to be seen. His plan was working—too well. The red dress she'd chosen with the idea of making Conner sorry he'd planned the evening clung to her body like a second skin. The moment they stepped into the restaurant, she'd regretted her decision. But it was too late to back down now.

"I like your dress," Conner whispered. "All you need to complete the look is a pair of those long red gloves and a cigarette holder."

Erica blanched and smoothed an imaginary wrinkle from her skirt. "What look?"

"The Dragon Lady. Isn't that what you had in mind when you picked this dress?"

She wasn't sure he'd caught on to her plan until she saw the hungry look in his eyes. Her trick had backfired. Conner pulled out a chair and waited for Erica to take her seat.

"I did not expect you to . . ." she began in a sharp voice. "I intended to look—"

"Desirable?"

He gave her a quick kiss behind one ear and settled into the chair across the table. "It worked. I like it better than the other two dresses you tried on."

"You were watching?"

"Of course. I take my protection duties seriously."

Before she let go with another tirade about his manipulation of her life, Erica accepted the menu offered to her and glanced at it. Their overly solicitous host identified their waiter and wine steward, then discreetly disappeared.

"I don't want to be Dragon Lady," she snapped. "I'm not even sure I want to be Erica Fallon. And stop hovering over me."

Conner opened his menu. "You don't like all this attention?"

"Your attention isn't free. I just don't know yet what it's going to cost."

"You're right, you don't."

A short time later, after he'd ordered for them in perfect Italian, Conner leaned across the table and smiled. "So, we'll give you another name. What about Gypsy? Or maybe one of the characters out of a Bond movie? What was that woman's name—Cat? Kitty?"

"Conner! Stop it." Erica lifted her wineglass and took a deep swallow. "This isn't a game."

"Ah, but it is. We're playing cat and mouse. I'm the cat and you're the cheese. We're waiting for the mouse to appear. And, unless I miss my guess, here he comes."

As a tall, rail-thin figure moved in their direction, Conner took Erica's hand, lifting it gallantly to his lips for a kiss.

"What are you doing?"

"Playing the part of a man in love, Erica. Hello, Kilgore, nice to see you."

Conner released Erica's hand as he stood to greet the man who was staring at them curiously.

"Preston? I thought that was you. I didn't know that you and Ms. Fallon were—friends."

"Oh, yes. Old friends. We met ten years ago in Berlin." He smiled at her.

"And what brings the two of you together again?" Brighton asked casually.

"We ran into each other recently in New York, at a party for the new international director of trade."

"I was out of the country then, but I heard it was quite an affair. I was sorry I missed it."

"Do join us, Kilgore."

"Yes. Please sit down, Mr. Kilgore," Erica added.

The man glanced across the restaurant, then pulled out a chair and took a seat. "Just for a moment. I have dinner guests. But please, call me Brighton. Committee meetings are business. Here we're all friends. What brings you two to New Orleans?"

Conner answered easily. "Why, Christmas, of course. We decided to get away for the holidays, spend some time together. Erica fancied someplace warm, and I had business here."

Kilgore pulled his gaze away from Erica. "Oh? What kind of business?"

"I'm searching for a very special piece of artwork. My client heard a rumor that you own it. I'm supposed to find out if you would consider selling it."

"And what piece is that?" Brighton asked.

"A statue of the Virgin Mary that disappeared during the German occupation of France during World War Two."

Kilgore suddenly looked at Erica. "I see."

Erica caught his quick frown before she leaned forward and smiled. "I told him you owned it, Brighton. I didn't think it was a secret. Was it?"

"Well, no, not really. But I expected anything we discussed in the committee to remain private, Erica."

"Oh, dear. I'm so sorry. I told Conner I'd ask

you to let us see it. I'm sure he won't say anything, will you, darling?"

"Of course not. Is the piece authentic?"

"Certainly," Brighton snapped, "I had it authenticated on delivery. The Virgin Mary may be my finest acquisition. I'm not interested in selling, but I'll be glad to show it to you while you're in New Orleans."

"Good," Conner said.

"Perhaps if you're successful in locating other pieces like it, you might allow me the opportunity to buy them. And"—he nodded at Erica—"our committee will be most interested in anything you learn."

"I thought you'd know where the statue came from."

"No, it came to me from a dealer who bought it from another dealer. You know how that goes. I've run into a dead end, even after offering to buy the information."

"For the committee, of course," Conner said.

"Of course. My wife and I are having a small dinner party tomorrow evening. Won't you join us? I think you'd enjoy touring our home, Erica. The architecture is very unusual. It's German."

"I'd love to see it, Mr. Kilgore."

"Now, now. It's Brighton, remember?" He stood and glanced across the restaurant. "I'd love to stay and talk art with you, but I really ought to get back to my guests. Why don't I have a car pick you

up in front at six-thirty? The house is about a half
hour's drive up river."

"We'll be ready." Conner reached out to shake
Kilgore's hand. "Until tomorrow night."

"Bring a wrap, Erica. Traditionally people along
the river build bonfires on the levee on Christmas
Eve. But the weatherman says that a storm will be
moving in, so we're lighting our bonfire a day
early."

"That sounds exciting." Erica shook his hand
and watched him walk away. She waited until her
racing pulse settled back down before she launched
into Conner. "Why did you tell him about Berlin?
Isn't that giving away too much?"

"I'm going to assume he already knew. If not,
he'll make it a point to find out. Either way, we've
offered them a connection to Berlin. It's up to him
or whoever is pulling the strings to make the next
move."

Their soup arrived, temporarily halting the discussion. Erica was glad of the distraction, but the
lump in her throat made it impossible for her to
enjoy the dinner. The false sense of intimacy he was
creating made her very uncomfortable. The vague
feeling of unease in her belly had turned into a
maelstrom of discomfort.

"Don't you like your soup?" he asked.

There was no way she would let him know how
his words had affected her. "It's very good." The
quiver in her voice threatened to give her away.
"I'm afraid I'm just not very hungry."

"Possibly because you're exhausted," Conner said with a quirk of his lips. "You didn't get much sleep last night."

He was more right than he knew. What sleep she had gotten came in little snatches between moments of observing Conner while he looked out the window. But there was no reason for him to know that. They'd better get back to business.

"I was an art history major, Conner. You probably know more about the missing pieces than I do," she said in dismay.

He gave her an unexpected slow grin that made the corners of his eyes crinkle and melted the frost in their icy blue color. "I don't know much about art, my Dragon Lady. But Sterling is an expert and keeps me fully informed."

He reached out and took her hand again. "It's going to be all right, Erica. I'll make it all right."

Erica didn't know if it was his smile or his words, but suddenly everything changed. Her shortness of breath disappeared and her appetite resurfaced. The waiter returned, removing the soup bowls and replacing them with large plates filled with thin slices of lamb and new potatoes. Erica glanced around.

In the soft light of the candles, the other diners disappeared. For now Erica let herself relax as much as she could in the light of Conner's solicitous attention. They'd be back in their suite much too soon, but she wouldn't allow herself to think about that. For now she would play her role in their charade of reunited lovers. And if she could make him uncomfortable, that would suit her just fine.

Lifting her eyes, she watched Conner take a lusty bite of his food and tried her own, surprised by the tenderness of the meat.

Conner finally spoke, interrupting her thoughts. "You may claim not to be an art expert, Erica, but I remember Bart raving about how bright you were."

That statement caught Erica by surprise. Bart had been a dedicated student, not given to loose praise. "I'm afraid your brother gave me more credit than I deserved. Truthfully, I never quite understood why he spent so much time with me."

"Because you were smart and dedicated. Bart valued hard work. I don't know why he ever put up with me. All brawn and no brains.

"Bart always said you had a big heart. He knew us both—very well."

Then, as if they'd reached some sort of unspoken agreement, they both smiled and turned to their food, finishing the meal with no further reference to either Brighton Kilgore or Berlin.

Only once did Conner refer to the past, when he asked, "So how'd you get from art history to politics?"

"You mean how'd I go to work for the ambassador? Actually, it happened by chance. I was in Paris when he was transferred there from Berlin. I'd been . . . ill." She focused her gaze on her plate. "Some friends dragged me to a party. It was the first time I'd been out in a long time. Ambassador Collins and I were introduced. He'd known my father. When he learned I was at . . . loose ends, he offered me a position as his assistant.

"I discovered I liked the work. Ambassador Collins's wife died. A man in his position needs someone to organize his social calendar as well as an administrative assistant. Being shot at isn't one of the usual job qualifications."

"You've been involved in the diplomatic community for the past ten years and this is the first time you've been in danger?"

"Threats are a part of the job when you're in foreign service, but they're not usually personal. What are you getting at?"

"Nothing," he said, entirely too casually. "I was just wondering why somebody decided to threaten you now."

"I've been thinking about that myself. Maybe it's because of the committee. I'm suddenly involved in a public search for lost art."

"I thought the committee had just been formed."

"We've had only one meeting, and it was an organizational one," she said. "I still can't believe what happened."

Neither could Conner. He didn't want to think that these incidents were tied to their relationship in West Berlin. He didn't want Erica to believe that either. "Maybe we're wrong about all this. Maybe this has nothing to do with what happened ten years ago. Could the book have something to do with the embassy?"

"If you're asking if the embassy has a little black book of spies and secret agents, sorry, no. And my personal address book is very dull. I don't see the connection. Unless . . ." She looked straight at Conner. "Unless I'm not the real target."

"It's too soon to know. And I hate not knowing what's going on around me. But let's don't worry about that tonight. What do we want for dessert?"

Erica pursed her lips and considered his question with more concentration than it warranted. "What I'd really like," she whispered, "is to get out of here, go for a walk, and do something normal like have some beignets and café au lait."

And work off some of the tension.

"Not a good idea, Erica. You know what happened before when you left the hotel."

"Conner, I do not intend to spend the rest of my life in hiding. Please?"

He was moved by the plea in her voice. Besides, after today's warning, they were probably safe, for tonight anyway.

"You're on." Conner signed the bill, stood, and pulled out her chair. It seemed only natural for him to touch her, guiding her through the restaurant and toward the elevator.

She stopped for a moment in front of the glass window overlooking the river. "It's so beautiful. Can we take the Moon Walk and watch the boats go by?"

"Not with you in that dress. They'd all crash. Let's change into something dark. And wear a cap or a scarf. Something to conceal your face."

In their suite, they separated to change. Erica stepped out of her silver slippers and red hose, then reached for the zipper at the back of the dress. Giving it a jerk, she felt it move for a second, then hang on something. Damn! What was it with her and zippers? The more she pulled, the worse it got. Why hadn't she bought the dress without a back?

Finally, she admitted defeat and opened her bedroom door. "Conner, could you give me a hand?"

Tugging on a sweater, he crossed the parlor and stopped in surprise. "You're still dressed."

"I—I can't seem to get my zipper open. Could—could you help me?"

"Of course." But the task proved more difficult than either expected. Finally, in exasperation, Conner gave a jerk to the tongue and Erica heard a rip.

"Oops."

"Conner, do you have any idea how much this dress cost?"

Now was not the time to let Erica know that he'd had its cost added to his bill. Instead, he tried to look humble as she caught its sides and held the garment up. "I'm so sorry, Erica. I'll have it repaired. Don't worry."

"I may just let you do it," she said, remembering the touch of his hands on her back. Her skin felt as if it had been fingerpainted with fire. "Now get out of here and let me dress."

"Are you sure you don't need some help with—with the stockings?"

"They're gone already. I can manage."

Erica hoped he couldn't hear the catch in her voice. To cool her heated skin she headed toward the closet, then turned to see what he was wearing.

Big mistake. Conner was dressed all in black, including the knitted cap that covered his blond hair.

She couldn't hold back a grin. "Are we pulling a caper later, boss?"

"I certainly hope so," he replied. "Remember, midnight is the witching hour."

A small boat decorated with a wreath and Christmas lights moved slowly along the bank. In the middle of the river a second boat sported a brightly lit Christmas tree with a star shining like a beacon in the darkness.

Erica drew in a deep breath as a quick little breeze danced across the Mississippi and caught her hair, dragging a strand from her braid and brushing it across her face. She shivered and crossed her arms over her chest.

"Cold?"

"A little. It's the dampness."

Conner slid his arm around her, drawing her close.

She struggled for a moment, until she felt the sharp jab of metal poking into her side. His gun. Even now he was prepared to defend her if need be. She'd never had anybody show this kind of concern for her. It made her feel humble.

"Once we get to the café, I'll be fine," she said.

"You're fine now," he said. "Listen." He stopped for a second.

"Christmas carols. Where is the music coming from?"

"Don't know. St. Louis Cathedral is ahead. Maybe they've opened it for services. Want to check it out?"

"Yes, let's."

They headed toward Jackson Square, where a crowd had gathered to listen to the carolers in front of the church.

The area between the iron fence that surrounded Jackson Square and the carolers was packed. Conner pushed Erica in front and stood behind her, sliding his arms around her waist to protect her from being jostled by the crowd.

Erica tried to put some distance between them, until she remembered the stranger in the street. Then she gave in to the need to be safe and nestled in Conner's arms, letting the sound of the music sweep over her.

When the singers launched into the lighter tunes like "Jingle Bells" and "Rudolph," the listeners clapped and joined in. Gradually the carolers grew more serious, ending their performance with

"Silent Night." Before the song ended, Conner drew Erica through the crowd and along the fence toward the French market.

"The Quarter never changes, does it?" Erica asked as they reached the French market with its giant Christmas tree decorated with fruits, vegetables, and bells. She could see the Café du Monde just ahead of the crowd.

"Not much. Years ago the city wrote up ordinances to keep the quarter just like it always was. Other than those already here, they even banned new neon lights, except on the first seven blocks of Bourbon Street."

"I didn't know that. I've only been here once—years ago."

"You've never been to Mardi Gras?"

"No, is that un-American?"

"Absolutely. When this is over, we'll—" His voice stopped short of the obvious completion of his sentence. "Look, our destination. And there's no line and there's a vacant table."

Quickly Conner made his way toward the small table with the two wrought iron chairs. The "we" had stopped him. Erica pushed aside any comment and directed her attention to the bustle of the customers lining up behind them to be seated.

Moments later he gave their order and before they could reclaim the intimacy they'd shared at the church, the waiter had returned with a tray holding two milky-white coffees and a platter of sugary confections. Erica took her cup and moved it in front of her, wondering where the closeness had gone.

She felt like a yo-yo, plunging from the highest mountains to the lowest valleys in a matter of moments.

Conner slid his chair nearer. "It's all right, Erica. You can relax. I'm not going to attack you."

She took a swallow of the steaming liquid and felt it burn the tip of her tongue. "I know."

"If it makes it easier for you, just tell yourself that this is all for show."

Erica glanced around. Conner was right. Her enemy could be watching right now. There was more at stake than a trip down memory lane with Conner Preston. The ambassador had already been wounded and only because of Conner's knowledge and quick reflexes had they escaped the second shooter. Erica had been given three warnings. Until they learned who was behind this bizarre plot, she had no choice but to go along with the charade. She certainly didn't have any better plan.

She could put some space between herself and Conner though. Once they got back to the hotel, she planned to insist on being moved to another room.

But an hour later, when they opened the door to the suite, the room had been completely ransacked.

SIX

"Wait here," Conner whispered, shoving her to the wall beside the open door and drawing his pistol. Like smoke he moved across the room, peering first into his room, then hers, then back again.

"It's okay."

But it didn't look okay. Pictures hung at an angle. Chair cushions had been tossed to the floor. Drawers were open with clothing spilling over the edges. Even the covers had been ripped off the beds.

The backs of Erica's knees turned to jelly, and she grasped a chair to support herself. "What were they looking for?"

"I don't know," Conner answered as he picked up the phone. "But a good guess is that they're still looking for the 'book.'"

"But I don't have any book. I don't know anything about a book. Conner, what are we going to do?"

"The first thing we're going to do is get another room for the night while security goes over this one." He cut his gaze back to the desk as he spoke into the phone. "Security, this is Conner Preston. We've had an intruder. Get up here and bring the manager."

Half an hour later, they'd been moved into another suite and a guard had been stationed outside the door in the foyer.

Conner led Erica to the bedroom. "Take a nice hot bath and relax. I'll get you a nightgown."

"But—"

"You'll be safe here. I promise."

"You'll come back?"

"Of course. It's almost midnight." He gave her a tired and gentle smile before he left.

Erica looked around the new room, this time not noticing the lavish furnishings. She felt empty and strung out.

Maybe it was Conner's concern that brought back old memories and filled her with longings both new and old.

Longings she tried to ignore. That's the past, Erica, she told herself. And the past was gone. Berlin. Falling in love. Hot, passionate sex and laughter. Conner had loved her unconditionally, something she'd never had before. He'd offered her joy, made her feel cherished.

She'd worked all her life to make her parents

notice her. They never did. Then Conner came
along and changed her life forever. He never knew
about the lonely, frightened woman she'd been. All
he saw, accepted, and loved was the person she became with him. But that was over. The only important thing now was the present, she assured herself
as she fought off the memories.

She didn't even want to think about her flight to
Paris, wondering if Conner had lived or died. She'd
told Conner's commander where she would be.
Then the long wait for him to come to her began.
When she found out about the baby, and became
very ill, she wrote to Conner, in care of the base.
For the first time her faith in her ability to survive
had been tested.

Time passed, Conner never came. Then she'd
lost their baby and been thrown into a state of darkness. For a long time she stopped caring whether
she lived or died or if he ever came back for her.
The loss of her child devastated her more than even
the death of her parents.

When she'd lost her mother and father, she'd
grieved. But they'd always been two steps away
from being gone anyway. As a child, she'd recognized their inability to live normal lives and be normal parents. Her mother was taught that the rich
would inherit the earth. And she'd expected it.
When the money she inherited from her family was
gone, her life became a desperate whirlwind of lost
opportunities and broken dreams.

In the end they'd ignored Erica, not from unkindness, but from ineptitude. They dealt with her only when etiquette and necessity demanded it. Erica simply blended into the luggage and the furniture. She remained quiet and studied hard, waiting for praise that never came.

Then her parents died in a car accident, and in a perverse twist of fate the insurance policy her aunt had taken out on them when Erica was born paid off. Accidental death. Double the amount for both parents. The money had freed Erica to have the kind of life her parents had always wanted. Except she couldn't. The memory of being without was always too close. So she invested the money and continued to live as if it weren't there. Even after their deaths, Erica fought for their approval. Through it all she studied, eventually earning the Fulbright Scholarship and her year of schooling in Germany.

Eventually, being a Fallon got her a job with the ambassador. Since then, hard work and a talent for foreign affairs had kept it.

Erica rolled her shoulders and closed her eyes. She was exhausted both physically and emotionally. A shower sounded good. A shower and sleep. Wearily she made her way to the bathroom and turned on the water. Peeling off her clothes, she stepped beneath the sting of scalding hot water. Tonight she still felt cold.

Using the expensive soap provided by the hotel, she lathered herself and washed her hair. Almost asleep on her feet now, she rinsed off and stepped from the shower, reaching for the plush robe hanging on the back of the bathroom door.

Toweling as much water as she could from her hair, she pulled a brush through its strands until the tangles were gone, wrapped a dry towel around her head, and padded barefoot toward the bed.

Moments later, when Conner entered the room, she was sound asleep on top of the covers, her robe tied loosely at the waist, pulled open in a V that revealed her bare knees and one thigh.

She was draped across the satin comforter like a Vargas girl from some pinup calendar. The soft luminescence from the lamp by the bed painted her with innocence.

Conner stood at the foot of her bed, watching her, wondering what secrets she was hiding behind that beautiful face. Did she know what book her assailants were looking for? Did she have it? If so, why didn't she tell him? Was the book connected to Bart's death?

Then Erica moved, the tie on her robe loosening and exposing her breasts. He hadn't often seen her sleep. Ten years ago sleeping would have been a waste of time. After their first time together, Erica had been lusty and wild in bed, willing to experiment, to follow any direction he'd led her. Even now he could still feel the promise of that heat. He cursed himself for wondering if he could bring it to life again. Only the memory of Bart had kept his passion at bay. Now Erica was soft and vulnerable in sleep, and he felt himself harden.

Drawing on every ounce of his control, Conner forced the memory of Bart and his own wounded body back to his mind. But this time it was slow to come and a different kind of anger flared inside him. He dropped the nightclothes he'd brought her at the foot of the bed and backed out of the room.

Special Forces training had served Conner well through the years, but no amount of training could prepare his body to resist her. He could detach himself from almost anything. He had. But Erica Fallon was his weakness and guilt over that weakness assaulted whatever anger he'd drawn about him as his shield.

It was time to check in with Mac again.

This time the phone rang longer and the voice that answered seemed tired.

"Mac? You okay?"

"Yes. You?"

Never a man to waste words, Mac waited for Conner's confirmation and launched into his report. "The base commander in Berlin was killed in a boating accident five years ago. All military records of the incident at the church have disappeared, or were never recorded. So far I haven't been able to find anyone else who was involved. I've talked to the minister of the church, but I'm afraid all he knows is what you know. The two men who came to the church were very nervous. They tied him up—I didn't know that before—and tore up the church, but they didn't even rob the poor box. He had the opinion that they knew who was coming and were following specific orders, but that's all he knew. Incidentally, he's sending you a wedding gift. It's being forwarded to Erica's home in Tennessee."

"Erica mentioned a gift. I can't believe he still had it," Conner said.

"He didn't know what to do with it."

Conner didn't know how he felt about that. It was a connection to the past he'd rather forget.

"And you're sure nobody ever got a letter from Erica?"

"Not that I've been able to learn. None were ever forwarded to Shangrila."

"What about Brighton Kilgore? How'd he get on the committee?"

"Money. Conner, the man made a fortune by turning a small chemical business into a very big company. He fancies himself a philanthropist. Funding the operation of the committee buys him prestige in the art world."

"And the statue? Where'd he get it?"

"Officially, he bought the statue from a dealer who has black market connections but who seems to have acquired it legitimately. Unofficially, who knows?"

Conner groaned. "And by providing the money for the committee, Kilgore puts himself in a position to get first crack at whatever they find. Can he do that? Own stolen property?"

"Not legally. Though there are loopholes. The French government is less likely to make a claim if he is responsible for finding other lost treasures."

"And anything he conceals from the public is his. Mac, what about Karl Ernst?"

"Ah—Mr. Ernst is a bit more interesting. He was, of course, on the teaching staff of the university both Erica and Bart attended and, as you know, Bart's adviser. If the relationship was anything more than a normal student-teacher one, I haven't been able to prove it."

Conner rubbed his eyes, pinching the bridge of his nose. "And since?"

"He's advanced steadily in the academic community, and continues to work with the reconstruction and preservation of historic buildings. Once the Berlin Wall came down, he was appointed as director of antiquities for the new German government. He lost his entire family during World War Two and his wife a few years ago. Likes power. Very ambitious."

Conner hadn't really expected Mac to learn much. Secretly, he'd already conducted his own unsatisfactory investigation without learning anything more. "Well, that puts us right back where we started, Mac. What about the gunman who took a shot at Ambassador Collins?"

"No trace. The bullet came from a Beretta. And every street crook has that kind of weapon now. The only way we could identify the bullet is by finding the weapon."

In his pocket, Conner felt the spent bullet he'd retrieved from the wall in Erica's house on Lookout Mountain. He'd dug it out while she was collecting the coffee and food and moving it into the office. He didn't need to have it analyzed to know it came from the same gun.

"Someone shoved Erica on the street today, Mac. He could have pushed her into traffic, but he didn't."

"Was she hurt?"

"No. He was just letting us know that he's around. What I'm more worried about is that our suite was searched—not for show. It's pretty obvious that they mean business about finding this book."

"And Erica doesn't have it?"

"That's the one thing I'm reasonably sure of," Conner admitted.

"And neither does the ambassador," Mac added.

"And neither do I. That leaves Kilgore and Ernst. We're going to a party at Kilgore's house tomorrow night. I think maybe Shadow will have to do a little private looking."

"I don't like the way this is going. Be careful, Conner."

"One final thing, Mac. What do you think about the ambassador?"

"I think he's scared."

Scared. That was interesting. Even Erica didn't appear to be scared. Neither had Bart. He could still see him holding out one hand toward the men wearing the ski masks. That picture would be burned forever in Conner's mind.

Bart had been at the church, standing by the

door, when Conner arrived. He'd already been antsy about the wedding. Erica's delay had only aggravated Conner's nerves.

How like a woman, he thought, to be late for her own wedding. He'd followed Bart into the church, right into the path of two men with drawn guns. They said something in German, which Conner couldn't understand.

In front, Bart knelt down and held up one hand while he reached inside his jacket. "Don't! Stop!"

The shot came unexpectedly, almost as if the man with the gun hadn't intended to fire. Before Conner realized what was happening, Bart crumpled to the ground, a look of surprise on his face, his life draining from the bullet hole in his neck.

"No!" Conner screamed, drawing his weapon. But before he could get off a shot, the sharp sting of a bullet tore into his right thigh. Then another, in his left leg, brought him down.

From somewhere outside, the church bell started ringing.

The men yelled at each other, then took off out the back door, and Conner dragged himself toward Bart.

But it was too late.

In the doorway of the church, as his blood dripped into Bart's, Conner railed out at God. How could this have happened? What good was Conner and all his special training if he couldn't have saved his brother's life? Now the only way he could get to the truth was to protect the woman he'd spent ten years blaming for his brother's death.

Conner checked the door to the suite. The hotel security guard was sitting outside. But Conner didn't fool himself. If somebody wanted to get in, the guard would prove only a small deterrent. Wearily he walked back to the parlor. He removed his pistol from beneath his sweater and laid it on the floor beside the couch where he intended to sleep. Conner punched up one of the pillows and stretched out. At least from this spot he'd be able to see anybody who came in. But it was going to be a long night.

It was morning. Erica's eyes felt dry, scratchy from the residue of salty tears that had never fallen. She listened quietly as she struggled to wakefulness.

Silence. Dragging herself to a sitting position, she looked down at the robe hanging open over her bare body. She hardly remembered leaving the bathroom.

She stood up, running her fingers through her snarled mass of hair. At the foot of her bed she saw a silky splash of color. Her nightgown and underwear. Left by Conner at some time during the night. He'd come into the room while she was sleeping.

A flush of heat burned her face. He'd seen her partially nude.

When she opened the door, Conner came instantly awake and lay watching her from the sofa. His hand had automatically curled around his pistol, but he didn't speak.

"Why didn't you sleep in your bed?" Her voice almost hoarse with tightness.

"What kind of bodyguard would I be behind a closed door?"

"Dangerous." Sexy, she thought as she took in his bare chest and unbuttoned jeans riding low on his hips.

"You'd be right."

They stared at each other for a minute. She, aware of the plush fabric of her robe brushing against her breasts as she breathed. He, making no attempt to cover himself.

He didn't trust her, but he was protecting her. And she was standing there, staring at his body and thinking about what might have happened at midnight.

If she hadn't fallen asleep.

Quickly she whirled and padded to her open suitcase, her clothing spilling over the edge into the chair on which it had been placed. She gathered up an armful of clothing and dashed back into her room, pausing at the door. "Thank you, Conner." She slid inside, closed the door behind her, and took a long, ragged breath.

She showered again, taking her time, more to put out the heat of her desire than from need. Wetting her hair once more, she finger-combed it, then spent long, empty minutes drying it before she pulled on a ruby-red cotton turtleneck shirt, a pair of jeans, and a matching patchwork vest. She was forced to don the socks and running shoes she'd worn the night before. Finally, she'd used up as much time as she could. Without makeup, she was as ready to face Conner as she'd ever be. Drawing in a deep breath, she opened the door.

At some point Conner had ordered room service. A waiter was uncovering dishes of fruit, eggs, and muffins.

"Just in time," Conner observed, running his fingers through still damp hair as he pulled out a chair.

He wore faded jeans and a sapphire-blue sweater that matched his eyes. He was suddenly the golden boy Erica had loved so deeply before the memory had been ripped from her heart. But that was a boy and this was a man. Erica shivered.

"Well? Aren't you hungry?"

She was still staring. Even the waiter noticed and smothered a grin. "Yes. Yes, I'm hungry."

Erica allowed herself to be seated, so chagrined at being caught looking at Conner that she missed Conner's head tilting down. When he brushed her lips with his, Erica couldn't hold back a gasp.

"Stop it, Conner."

"Oh, that's all right, darling." He glanced at the waiter. "He won't tell anyone that we're in love, will you?"

Damn him. He was deliberately doing this, and she couldn't refuse.

"Did you have a good night?" he whispered as his lips trailed away from her mouth and behind her ear and back to her lips again.

Erica leaned toward him until she realized what she was doing and stopped herself. She had to go along with their pretense as lovers, but she didn't like Conner having the upper hand. And most of all, she didn't like an audience. But she could give as good as she got.

"Of course, darling," she said sweetly, returning his kiss with as much passion as she dared give. "When I'm with you I always have a good night. What about you?"

Conner looked at her for a moment. Her play-acting was all the invitation he needed. Knowing she couldn't back away, he lowered his face again, taking her lips with heart-stopping thoroughness.

Forgetting the hotel employee for a moment, she felt a familiar dreamy pleasure wash over her. Her body went weak as a hot flush of desire ignited and raced through her.

Then the waiter coughed, drawing them back to the present. Conner gave a reluctant sigh and pulled away. He took the bill and signed it, then sat down at the table, watching the door close behind the waiter.

"What do you think you're doing?" Erica demanded furiously.

"Kissing you. And rather thoroughly. Only," he said wickedly, "in answer to your invitation."

"Don't do that again."

"As I recall, it was a mutual endeavor. Don't worry, Erica. I won't take your invitation seriously. We both know we had an audience."

She tried to cover her still-racing pulse with a calm demeanor. "Did I play my part all right?"

"Oh, you know how to play, darling. You always did. What would you like, Erica?"

"Am I allowed to say?"

"To eat, darling. What may I serve you?"

Satisfied that her kiss had rattled him as much as it had her, she backed off and admitted to herself that what she'd like was to retreat into her room and slam the door. His show-and-tell had turned into more of a game of hit and run and she suspected she was the most wounded. She swallowed hard and forced her attention to the dishes. Strawberries. Melon. Fluffy yellow eggs. Crispy bacon and—"chocolate-chip muffins?"

"I told you yesterday, I have a weakness for chocolate."

"Yes. I remember. After midnight."

"Exactly. I could tell you didn't share my cravings."

"Really? What gave you that impression?"

"At the witching hour you were sound asleep."

"You had no business being in my room." Erica couldn't imagine what kind of picture she must have presented, sprawled across the covers, half nude. She blushed.

"I knocked but you never answered. Considering what's happened so far, I decided I'd better make sure you were all right."

"Was I?"

"Oh, yes, Dragon Lady. You were incredible. I was tempted to kiss you awake to share my treat."

"What treat?"

"Chocolate, of course. But that's all right. I'm always prepared. Have a muffin."

SEVEN

By mid-morning Erica was going crazy from inactivity. Conner spent the morning in his own room on the phone with Sterling. He told her it was Paradox, Inc. Business, but Erica had her doubts.

Finally she retreated to her room, pacing and thinking, asking herself more questions than she had answers for. Most frustrating of all were her feelings for Conner.

Having him touch her was sheer hell. It was all she could do to keep from giving away her heated response. He was the most attractive man she'd ever known, but it was more than that. She was still in love with him. And she was afraid that if she weren't careful, she'd end up like she had ten years ago—hurt and alone.

No, she was a different woman now. She'd survived his belief that she'd betrayed him, his callous desertion. She wouldn't let that happen again. She'd look at the relationship for what it was—a grand masquerade, a hoax, a charade. Sure she would. All she had to do to accomplish that was wear eye patches and stuff cotton in her ears.

No, she'd call Mac. Insist that he send someone else. Demand another room. Leave New Orleans.

Then she heard a knock on the door and Conner's voice asking, "Ready for some lunch?" And all her resolutions committed hara-kari in her stomach.

"Just as long as it's not chocolate."

"Aren't you worried about leaving the hotel in the daytime?" Erica asked as Conner moved her through the front hotel entrance and onto the sidewalk.

"Not now. The person looking for the book is convinced that you're the key to finding it. He isn't going to hurt you and lose his source. Besides I'm with you. And I'm ready for him."

And he was. She could see the steely determination in his eyes, the concentration, the total awareness of everyone and everything around them.

"Where are we going, Conner?"

"To the Napoleon House, a little bar in the middle of the French Quarter."

"A little early for liquor, isn't it?"

"Not liquor, muffuleta."

"Fine," Erica agreed, glad to be out of the hotel. She was fond of the Cajun sandwich.

They walked through the narrow streets of the French Quarter, dodging garbage cans filled with refuse from the night before and a patron or two still sleeping off the results of whatever he'd been celebrating.

Neat private residences were tucked between the dingy little shops. They passed a woman wearing a white apron, her hair covered with a three-cornered print handkerchief like some servant from the time the house was built. She was sweeping dirt down a tiny sidewalk and through the fence opening into the street. Beside the walk a dark red camellia bush was in full bloom. Erica smiled. In spite of her trauma of the night before, the morning sun was warm and the day bright and invigorating.

Conner led them across the street out of the sunlight toward a building on the corner that was so dark and dingy, Erica drew back. "This is where we're going?"

"Yep."

"But the walls look as if they're about to fall and there isn't even a sign."

"Yep. That's why I come here in the daytime. You really have to know where you're going to find it at night. Come on, you'll like it, I promise." Minutes later they were sharing a monstrous sandwich of meats and cheeses on a huge round bun. It was a relief to be making normal small talk without playing out their charade or discussing missing books. But more than that, it was nice to be with Conner again, exploring dark, dingy little bars, enjoying good food and each other.

Yes, he still liked motorcycles.

And, yes, she still cried over animals and—she couldn't bring herself to say babies, finishing with old movies, instead.

"What kind of man is the ambassador?" Conner asked.

"He's very dedicated. I think he had a hard time when he was young. He came from a poor family. Getting where he is wasn't easy. You know, he was appointed by Nixon and has served every president since."

"I didn't know that." In fact, neither he nor anybody else knew much about Collins. He was one of those people who did his job quietly and was constantly overlooked. "Where else have you been posted other than Paris?"

"Just here in the States. He's on temporary assignment at the United Nations, but that may change. He isn't sure where they'll send him next."

"Is there somewhere else he'd like to go?"

Erica took a long time to consider that question. "He's never said. But if he could pick and choose, I think he'd really like to go back to Berlin. His wife was German."

"She was?" Conner leaned forward and took Erica's hand. He hadn't known that and he couldn't think of any bearing it might have to their search. But he liked holding Erica's hand. He liked looking at her and having her smile back.

The locals, gathered at the bar, cast curious glances at two strangers who were so obviously enjoying themselves.

When their plates were empty, the waiter brought a tray containing two icy sherbets. "Compliments of the house," he explained. "For two lovers on this most special holiday."

"But we aren't—" Erica began to say.

"Thank you," Conner interrupted, taking Erica's hand. "This is a very special time."

They ate the fruity ice with relish. Their hosts were right. Erica knew it was a special time and she'd stopped examining the reasons or the ramifications. Today just was.

Tomorrow would take care of itself.

Later, as they walked the streets on the way back to the hotel, it seemed only natural to hold hands. They stopped in a small shop, where Conner bought Erica a sequined carnival mask with feathers. Erica bought Conner a voodoo doll complete with a long, wicked pin. They laughed and said it was the man behind their troubles and they ought to give it a jab in the heart.

They stopped on the street and watched a small boy tap-dancing for tips, ate sticky pralines, and took a ride in a carriage pulled by a horse wearing daisies on her hat.

For now they were content to be Conner and Erica, who were getting to know each other again.

At the end of their ride, Conner helped Erica

out of the carriage and glanced at his watch. "I hate to end this, but it's getting late."

Erica looked at her own watch and grimaced. "Goodness. If I'm going to be ready for Brighton Kilgore's party, we'd better hurry."

Conner took her hand once more and started back toward the hotel. "How about that red dress?"

"You destroyed it, remember? Besides, that dress wouldn't be appropriate." She knew he hadn't understood her choice of that dress and explaining could change the tone of the mood they'd captured. "It's too—too bold."

"Not for me."

This time Erica followed her own taste and dressed in a simple black sheath with cap sleeves and a fitted skirt that stopped just above her knees. This time her hose were black sheers and her shoes were simple black pumps with hourglass heels. Obsidian stones set in antique silver graced her ears and matched the oversize pin on the dress. Satisfied that she'd pass inspection, Erica remembered the bonfire and reached for a fringed black woolen stole that would cover almost her entire body.

Tucking a lipstick and small comb in a postage-stamp-sized evening bag, she glanced at her watch and left the room.

If her dress were one of understatement, Conner's gray Armani suit and matching silk shirt were a statement. Donald Trump would have envied the man she was seeing. His only concession to the brash young Conner she'd known were the tiny cream-colored hearts on his red tie.

She took a long look at the tie and smiled. "A bit early for hearts, isn't it?"

"Well, I can't wear my heart on my sleeve, so I've put it somewhere else. Besides, these aren't hearts, they're ornaments."

"Sure, and I'm the tooth fairy."

"Damn! My mother told me the tooth fairy would come only if I were asleep. Just think what I missed for a few lousy quarters."

That exchange set the tone for the evening. The chilled champagne waiting inside the polished black limo in front of the hotel simply continued Conner's illusion that they were two lovers celebrating having found each other again.

The driver closed the window between them and they were left in soft darkness, the only illumination coming from two lights over the bar.

"I suppose you're used to this kind of travel," Conner said. "Ambassadors tend to go for show."

"Like you?" Erica countered. "I mean Conner Preston doesn't drive himself, does he?"

"He does. Unless he has no choice. That way I'm in control of when I come and when I go."

Control, that was the key. Conner Preston would always have to be in control. Was that really such a bad thing? So long as the person in control was kind and caring, did it really matter?

Erica answered her own question. Yes. It did

matter. For too many years she'd been controlled by disinterest and omission. Once she lost the baby, Erica had done what she should have done long before; she changed the direction of her own life. She'd had enough school to last forever. She knew a little bit about a lot of things, but nothing consumed her. Now she wanted the security of being cared for.

For the last years her life had been neatly defined. She lived in the embassy. She worked in the embassy and she liked both. The dinner tonight was no different from a hundred others she'd attended. She would be interesting and she'd find a way to get what she needed from the other guests. She was good at that.

Except tonight, she was with Conner.

Conner uncorked the champagne and filled two glasses. He held one out to Erica. She took it, holding it in both hands so that he wouldn't see how her hands were trembling. Taking his own, he lifted it in salute.

"To us, Erica. Shadow and his Dragon Lady."

"Yes," she murmured, touching her glass to his. "Together again."

EIGHT

The driver wound his way north on River Road. Erica looked out the window, but not only was it too dark, the levee was too high for her to see the Mississippi beyond it.

Soft music played from the tape deck. They drank their champagne with no conversation. Until—"Conner?"

"Yes?"

"You—you never married?"

He hadn't expected the question. Marriage had meant Erica. When that didn't happen, he'd never let any relationship go that far again. To cover the awkwardness of an answer, Conner drained his glass and placed it in the rack on the bar. Then, as if in slow motion, he took her glass and added it to the rack. Finally he reached out and drew her small hand between his larger ones. "No. There have been women, but I've never married, never even come close. You?"

There was a tightness about his answer that made her sorry she'd asked. Now that he'd answered, she was left with giving some kind of response, and she had none. In her own life there'd been men—a few, but never close enough to consider a permanent relationship.

For minutes they'd been staring at each other, neither ready to carry the thought further. "No," she finally said, then to cut off any more questions, she said, "I mean I wouldn't want Mr. Kilgore to think that I would become—intimate with a married man."

"I'm sure such a thought would never occur to him." Conner swallowed a smile. It seemed his Erica had turned into an old-fashioned girl. She hadn't been a virgin when they'd met, but she'd been inexperienced. Like a flower slowly opening, every time they were together he learned something new. But they'd met and fallen in love so fast and furiously that they never had a chance to get to know each other the last time.

Now she was worried about her reputation, or maybe it was his. He liked that. Yes, Conner was learning a great deal about this new Erica. But the thing he was most intrigued with was that the new Erica and the old Erica were the same person. They always had been. And God help him, he wanted them both.

Moments later the car turned off the narrow

black-topped road and into a long tree-lined drive. Erica drew her hand away and laid it on the plush fabric along the base of the tinted windows. "Look at the lanterns," she said, pointing to the festive lights hung between two lines of ancient oaks, welcoming them to the estate. Only when they exited the drive and moved around the branches of a giant magnolia tree did the house come into view.

Not house, castle. Erica burst out laughing, then caught back the sound with her hand. "My goodness. He wasn't kidding when he said it was different."

The structure was a German castle, a fortress made of stone with turrets at the corners. It might have overlooked the Rhine River instead of the Mississippi. The only thing missing was a moat and a drawbridge.

Conner shook his head. "I can't believe it started out looking like this. I think our host has taken a few liberties in his restoration."

The driver opened the limo door and assisted them to the steps of the ornate mansion. Brighton Kilgore himself came through the door to meet them.

"Come in. Come in. Everyone here is most eager to meet you."

They found the drawbridge, skillfully recreated in the foyer. Beyond the simulated wooden planks a slim, blond-haired woman headed toward them. "Mr. Preston. Miss Fallon, welcome! I'm Lillian

Kilgore. Come into the Great Hall and meet our other guests."

Once Erica got past the shock of a German castle on the banks of the Mississippi, she noticed the old wall hangings, the swords and torches that had been converted to gas. Unless she missed her guess, all were authentic to the time period and surroundings. Brighton Kilgore might be a showoff spending his new money to buy his position in the art world, but Erica had to hand it to him, he certainly knew his antiques.

"Do you get the feeling that we've stepped back in time?" Conner whispered in amusement. "He's really worked at it. I'll bet he has a dungeon."

"Yes. And he's done a pretty good job of making it an authentic trip."

"I was afraid you were going to tell me that."

Other guests were already gathered around a fireplace big enough to roast an entire cow and leave room for a couple of small pigs. A roaring fire provided welcome heat for the room whose ceiling vanished into shadows above.

"Everyone," Mrs. Kilgore said, "come and meet Conner and Erica." She introduced two local couples Conner had never met before, then said, "Erica, I believe you know Karl Ernst?"

Erica caught back a sound of surprise. "Of course. Mr. Ernst, this is my—my friend, Conner Preston."

Conner's first impression of the German art expert was one of surprise. Karl was short and round, hiding a double chin beneath a goatee.

"Mr. Preston. It's my very great pleasure to know you. Of course I've heard a great deal about Bart's brother."

There was a sudden silence, as if all the guests had inhaled at once.

"Did we meet when I was stationed in West Berlin?" Conner asked, knowing that they never had.

"I don't think so. But your brother was very proud of you. I think he envied you your free spirit. I'm so sorry about what happened to him. There was a certain amount of unrest when the decision was made to reunite Berlin. After you returned to the States, several other American soldiers were attacked. It was a bad time for those of us who lived there and others caught up in the change. How is the ambassador, Erica?"

"He's improving, thank you," she answered, confused over his unexpected presence. "I didn't know you were coming to New Orleans, Mr. Ernst."

"I hadn't planned to. When Mr. Kilgore learned that I would be celebrating Christmas alone in New York, he insisted that I come home with him."

"So you're an old bachelor like me?" Conner asked.

"I am. After I lost my wife, I never remarried. I greatly regret that we had no children."

"A personal sorrow we, too, share," Brighton

concurred. "When I bought this house, I'd thought it would be a fine place for a family."

Conner wasn't sure about that. It would have scared the hell out of him. He expected some gargoyle to leap down from the balcony above at any minute.

Brighton Kilgore beckoned to his servant, who brought a tray with a bottle of wine, two glasses, and hors d'oeuvres. Erica declined the wine, but did take one of the small biscuits filled with seafood.

The final member of the dinner group was a stranger to Erica. A man, standing with Karl Ernst. As Erica caught his eye he gave her an odd little smile that seemed to suggest they shared a joke. If she'd had to describe him, she couldn't have found one outstanding characteristic that would make him memorable. He was quite simply average, until Brighton called him over.

"William, come and meet our other guests. Erica, Conner, this is William Boykin, my secretary. He's another orphan."

"Very nice to meet you, ma'am. I've heard a great deal about you. Is New Orleans your home?"

For a moment Erica could only stare. She didn't know the man, but the voice was familiar. She'd heard it before. Where?

"Eh, no. Do you live here?"

He laughed. "No, I guess you'd say home is where I hang my hat. Mr. Preston?" He nodded and gave a half-bow.

Karl Ernst took Erica's elbow. "Have you seen

Brighton's Christmas tree? It's an authentic old world tree. You know that Christmas trees came to this country from Germany?"

"No. I don't think I did," Erica answered, allowing herself to be led over to the tree at one end of the room. It was real, a fir. The paper and porcelain ornaments were very old. But the lights made the tree exceptional. In Germany the candles on the end of each branch would be made of wax. But in the spirit of safety, Brighton had used electric candles. Only close examination revealed that they weren't authentic.

"I never had a tree when I was growing up," Erica admitted. "We always seemed to be traveling or visiting someone else. It's very beautiful, Mrs. Kilgore." Erica turned to Karl Ernst, who still stood at her side.

"Thank you," Mrs. Kilgore replied. "By the way, where did the ambassador disappear to? My consulate wanted to send flowers, but he'd left the hospital."

"He's staying with . . . friends," Erica explained.

Mrs. Kilgore came to stand beside Erica. "Such a lovely dress," she murmured. "Understated elegance. I see you, and I wish I were young again and petite."

Mr. Ernst moved back toward the fireplace and the other men. Erica gave a light laugh and wished she were standing with them instead of her hostess.

"But you're so nice and tall. I'll bet you were once a model."

She was rewarded with a warm blush. "Well, I did do some catalogue work for a lingerie company. But when Brighton and I married, he insisted that I give that up. Not suitable for the wife of a man on his way to the top."

"I know Brighton is in the chemical business now," Erica said. "Was he always?"

"Oh, no. He was with the government when we met. He was an inspector of some sort. He investigated companies who broke the law."

"Like a detective?"

"Something like that. Then he bought into one of the companies he inspected. Straightened it out and now he owns it."

Erica accepted another hors d'oeuvre from the circulating waiter.

Across the room she could see Conner and Brighton Kilgore talking. Her eyes were automatically drawn to Conner. He stood out like a polished jewel honed to perfection with an icy exterior that never quite concealed the raw fire inside. As she watched, he glanced up, their gazes melding.

Just like in the song, across a crowded room. And she knew. Nothing had changed. She was as much in love with him now as she had been ten years ago, when he'd let her down. No matter what resentment she still harbored, that fact didn't change. He hadn't answered her letter. He hadn't cared enough to give her a chance to explain. If he'd wanted to come back to her, nothing would have stopped him. The Conner she knew then would have said to hell with any warning she'd been given. She was his woman and nobody would keep them apart.

Why hadn't he?

Because of Bart.

It always came back to Bart's death and her responsibility for it. At least in Conner's mind. She pulled her gaze away, searching for something to focus on. Even if they did discover what happened, it wouldn't change Conner's lack of faith in her. It wouldn't bring back her trust in him.

As if he sensed her thoughts, Conner broke away from the men and headed toward her. Only the waiter's announcement that dinner was served kept Erica from turning and rushing out the door.

Mrs. Kilgore intercepted Conner and took his arm possessively. "Come along, Mr. Preston. You're going to sit beside me and tell me all about that lovely company you have. I intend to commission you to spend lots of my husband's money on a piece of jewelry I heard about."

"I'll be glad to. Your husband told me he has acquired a new piece of artwork for his gallery, the Virgin Mary," Conner said with a smile. "I know he must be excited."

"Oh, yes. You have no idea. Personally," she confided, "I don't see the point in having something you can't put out for company. But he is positively ecstatic."

"I would be also. He's promised to show it to me."

She looked at him in surprise. "He did? I mean, he's usually so secretive about his collection. But then, fine art is your field, isn't it? Come, let us sit down."

Conner allowed her to direct him to the chair beside her. On the other end of the table, Kilgore was fussing over Erica.

Conner was beginning to wonder if bringing Erica had been wise. There were always unknown dangers in a search for the truth.

When that feeling of danger came to him previously, it acted like a catalyst for the senses. Everything was magnified. Colors were even more brilliant. Sounds were intensified. Paths became clearer. Skipping past the danger was second nature.

Except on the morning Bart was killed. The color and the senses were there, but not as harbingers of danger. Every part of him had been focused on Erica. He hoped that he wasn't making that mistake again.

The meal was a surprise. Rich, pungent gumbo, red beans and rice, were washed down by great pitchers of beer.

"You know," Mrs. Kilgore explained, "many of the Cajuns were actually Germans. They were more accustomed to eating turnips, cabbage, and potatoes, which were in short supply here. But the baron, the merchant who built our castle, apparently had an African housekeeper who quickly converted the family to the local fares. We thought you might enjoy a typical Louisiana feast."

"Of course, if we really wanted to be typical," Brighton interrupted, "we'd be serving you salt pork, corn bread, rice, and wild turkey."

A twitter of laughter rose and fell.

Conner raised his goblet in a toast. "On behalf of your guests, I thank you for the delicious gumbo."

Erica took a spoon of the stew and silently agreed. She was often called on to take part in long-drawn-out official functions where chicken or beef was the main dish. This was turning out to be a pleasant surprise. She was seated between one of Brighton's neighbors and Karl Ernst. The opportunity was being presented to gather information on a social level and she ought to make use of it.

Turning a bright smile on the rotund little man, she asked, "Do you really think the committee will learn anything about the missing artwork?"

"It won't be easy," he admitted. "After all, unscrupulous treasure hunters have been searching for nearly fifty years. Some of them may even have had a part in hiding the stolen goods. My guess is that most of it was destroyed in the bombing of Berlin or melted down to pay war debts."

"Have any of the artworks been found?" Mr. Boykin asked.

Mr. Ernst spent no time acknowledging the secretary. All his attention was focused on Erica. "Some, yes. There was an American soldier who was part of the first team in after the surrender. He gathered up everything he could, packed it up, and sent it home. Only when he died and the family found the cache of paintings and religious icons did we learn it still existed."

Erica glanced down the table, wondering if Conner could hear, and decided that their hostess was doing a good job of preventing that. "That's illegal, isn't it?"

"Technically yes. But every invading army has done the same thing throughout history. The treasures probably didn't legally belong to the churches and museums that housed them in 1940. Hitler's troops claimed them as the spoils of war for the glory of the German Empire. Your soldier just looked at it as souvenir hunting. Same results."

"Like Bart's marble arm?" Erica asked.

A flash of surprise appeared on Karl's face, then disappeared just as quickly. "Bart's arm?"

"Yes. In one of those tunnels we were mapping out we ran across a piece of broken marble. Bart thought it was probably a piece of one of the statues behind the altar. Didn't he show it to you?" she asked.

Karl shrugged his shoulders. "Me? I'm afraid not. Bart came to me only once about anything out of the ordinary and that was the night before he died. He wanted to know about the police."

Down the table Conner turned his attention to Ernst, no longer pretending to listen to his hostess.

"The police?" Erica repeated. "Why would he ask you about the police?"

Karl took a bite of the beans and rice, chewing thoughtfully as he answered. "Apparently he was afraid he had been followed. He wondered what the police would do to a foreign student who broke the law."

"He didn't say what kind of law?" Erica asked.

"No. I told him not to worry. If I ever saw a student who was law-abiding, it was Bart. I got the idea he was asking for his brother." Karl glanced at Conner. "I understand that your—friend was pretty wild back then."

"What did you tell him?"

"I sent him to the American embassy. If he or Conner got into trouble, the consulate was his best ally."

The rest of the dinner passed uneventfully. But Erica was uncomfortable with what she'd learned. She'd been sure that Bart had told her he'd shown the piece of broken marble to his adviser, that Karl had even kept it. But it was so long ago, she might be remembering wrong.

Or was Karl Ernst lying?

Once the after-dinner coffee and liquors were served, Brighton tapped on his glass for attention. "Conner, are you and Erica ready to see my little collection?"

"We certainly are."

"I promised Ernst a look at her too. If you'll come along."

As Brighton flicked on the wall sconces, Conner and the others followed him up the stairs and down a corridor to a heavy locked door. On the side panel next to the door was an elaborate security system into which Brighton punched a series of numbers. Finally the door opened and Brighton entered, standing aside while his guests filed into the room.

Erica had been in many home galleries, but this one was unique. There was one long wall devoted to paintings, each with its own light above. The other wall displayed flat sculpture, photographs, lithographs, and other unusual pieces. But the table in the center was the focal point of the collection. Beneath a clear dome, drenched in soft light, was a small, intricately molded gold statue of the Virgin Mary standing on an ornately carved base. She was barely twelve inches tall. Her small face was so beautiful, every detail in the skin so realistically drawn that Erica expected to see her cry.

"She's exquisite," Conner whispered. "I can see why finding this would inspire such dedication to search for the rest of the treasures."

"Do we know the artist?" Erica asked.

Brighton smiled. "You tell me. You're the art historian."

Erica shook her head. "I'm afraid this was never included in any of my classes. Maybe Professor Ernst knows who the artist is."

"I don't," he replied. "Though I recall a description of such a piece in the list of missing treasures. There were two of them, identical. They came from a small chapel in France."

Brighton Kilgore beamed from ear to ear. "Isn't she extraordinary?"

"Extraordinary," Conner agreed. "Would it be possible for me—for Erica to have a photograph of the statue?"

"Yes," Erica added. "The committee needs to begin compiling a reference file."

Conner gave Erica a grateful smile. "I could have my office run a check on the photograph. I keep an extensive file of artists and pieces. For my work."

Brighton pursed his lips as he considered the request. "I suppose so. As long as it isn't released to the public. You see, I have a state-of-the-art security system, but I'd rather not test it. Joseph? Bring the Polaroid."

As Brighton made several snapshots of the statue, Conner and Erica gave lip service to what otherwise would be an enviable collection. By the time they'd covered the room, the pictures were ready and Conner stuck them inside his coat pocket.

"Now," Brighton announced. "Let us move to the levee, where we'll light our annual Christmas bonfire."

Conner spoke briefly with Mrs. Kilgore, then disappeared while topcoats and furs were donned. He rejoined the guests on the porch. Conner, Erica, and Brighton were three of the first six guests ferried by limo down the long drive and across River Road. Uniformed servants stood along the steps, holding lanterns to guide them to the top of the levee while the limo went back for the others.

"In the old days," Brighton explained, "the house was much closer to the water. But the Mississippi is a lady with a mind of her own. Until the Army Corps of Engineers built this levee back in the thirties, the river changed course every few years."

Conner was holding Erica's hand as they topped the grassy ridge and walked across the road-wide strip of gravel along the top. A blast of cold air swept in from the river, almost pushing her back. Conner pulled her closer, sliding his arms around her waist, enclosing her inside his topcoat next to his body.

"Thank you, Father West Wind," he whispered in her ear. "I've wanted to do this since dinner."

"What?"

"Hold you close. You look good enough to eat, and I had to satisfy myself with gumbo and rice. Pure torture."

"No gun tonight?"

Conner didn't mention the one strapped to his ankle. "No, if we're attacked, you'll have to defend me."

In the darkness, Erica allowed herself to lean against him, grateful not only for the warmth, but for the sense of belonging she'd felt ever since they'd arrived. Gradually her tightly drawn nerves began to relax, then tingle in subdued but definite excitement.

With his arms around her, Conner burrowed beneath her woolen stole and caught her wrist. "You're cold," he said.

"Only on the outside."

"Don't talk like that, Dragon Lady. You know what that does to me."

"What?"

"Makes me think of midnight and chocolate."

"Maybe if you speak to Mrs. Kilgore she'll brew you a cup of hot cocoa when we go back to the house."

"She'd better not."

Conner's fingers laced with hers, his middle finger drawing little circles in her palm. Viewing the Kilgores' Christmas tree earlier, she'd felt an unaccountable sadness for all the Christmases they had missed, she and Conner and the child he never knew he'd lost. Now she needed his touch. She wanted to know that he needed her. If just for this one night, she needed to feel wanted.

"This is some levee," she said, trying to distract herself from the sensations of his body and hands on her. "It's certainly nothing like the ones I saw on television when they were filling sacks with sand to hold back the flood waters."

"Ummmmm."

"It must be more than fifty feet across. It's like a dam."

"Ummmmm."

He slipped his other hand beneath her arm to her abdomen. Erica's heart, already beating rapidly, began to pound so hard that she was sure the others could hear it. Approaching footsteps announced the arrival of the rest of the guests.

"As you can see," Mrs. Kilgore was saying, "we have already constructed our frame. Bring the lanterns, Joseph, so that our guests can see what you've done."

As the servants moved toward the large, dark shape, there was a gasp of astonishment. The castle had been recreated in the eight-foot-high structure, even down to the turrets on the corners of the edifice.

"I see you're surprised," she went on. "Some of our neighbors build a simple cone shape from logs, driftwood, and sugarcane stalks. But most are more elaborate—boats, animals. In honor of our special guests this year, Brighton had our home recreated."

"Oh, my. I can't imagine that you'd want to burn this," one of the women observed.

"And Christmas Eve isn't until tomorrow," another voiced.

Privately Erica decided it was the height of conceit for a man to torch his home. Still, perhaps the symbolism was such that his gesture was one of warmth instead of ego.

Brighton took a torch and walked toward the castle. "True, but any bonfire tomorrow evening is likely to be drowned out by the rain. So we decided to light our fire tonight in honor of our guests."

"Where did the tradition originate?" Erica asked.

"Every year, on Christmas Eve, the people along the river build fires of welcome for Father Noel, who comes downriver in his pirogue to deliver gifts to the children. Another custom which is said to have originated in Germany."

"Joseph, bring the champagne," Mrs. Kilgore commanded.

After everyone was served, Brighton Kilgore lifted his glass. "To friends both old and new and to all those things that link the present with the past. Merry Christmas to one and all."

As they drank the icy liquid, Brighton lit the torch and touched it to the bottom of the replica of his castle. As they watched it burst into flames, as if on signal other bonfires were struck, lighting a path up and down the river.

"It's a beautiful tradition," Erica murmured. "If I were Father Noel, I'd bring everyone along the river wonderful gifts."

"What would you like Father Noel to bring you?" Conner asked Erica.

"Me? Don't be silly. My parents explained the myth to me when I was five years old. After that I pretty much gave up on gift-giving of any kind. I mean going into a store and buying your own Christmas present just isn't much fun."

She might have given up, but Conner didn't

have to be told that she hadn't given up the dream. Even he and Bart had held on to their belief in Santa as long as possible, "else," Conner had explained to the brother who was six years younger, "he won't come to see us anymore." He'd known Erica was an only child and she'd never shared any of her childhood experiences, except for the well-worn bunny on her bed. Now that he looked back on it, they'd spent all their time in the present.

The glasses were returned to the tray and Erica gratefully reclaimed her spot of warmth in Conner's arms. As the fire stretched toward the heavens, Conner remembered Erica's confession that she'd never had a Christmas tree. At that moment he resolved to give her a tree with all the trimmings, including a visit from Santa. Back at the house he excused himself and found a phone. He didn't have much time, but if you had money, an hour was long enough.

On the way back to the hotel later, Erica lay in the curve of Conner's arm, resting her cheek on his chest.

"Karl Ernst thinks that most of the treasures were destroyed by the bombing of Germany at the end of the war," Erica said.

"Could be." Conner planted a kiss along Erica's ear, then chastised himself for letting his pleasure interfere with her attempt at sharing information.

"Did you know about the American soldier who gathered up all the paintings and religious icons and shipped them home?"

He moved his lips lower. "I think I read something about it. He kept them in a bank vault, didn't he?"

"Until he died and his family discovered his secret."

"What else did Karl say?"

"He said that Bart only came to him once, the night before he died. He was worried about being followed. Professor Ernst said he sent Bart to the American embassy."

"You don't believe him?"

"It isn't that. It's just that I'm sure Bart told him about the piece of marble we found in that hidden room."

Conner stopped his assault on her face and listened. "You mean the elbow *we* found?"

"That's the one. Bart said that the professor kept it. At least I thought he did. Of course, I could be wrong. I did have something else on my mind."

"Something like this?"

The memory of past kisses made this one even more potent. Her response destroyed the tiny thread of control Conner had left. Without relinquishing his lips, Erica twisted around so that she was lying across him, giving him complete access to her neck.

But that wasn't enough. He wanted all of her, wanted to feel her purring beneath him, to plunge inside of her. She might want no part of him in her life, but, by God, she still wanted his body. He glanced up at the closed window in frustration. Taking Erica here, in the back of the limo, was not what he wanted.

He felt Erica's finger run down his cheek and across his chin, drawing his attention to her face. And then he saw it, the sweet smile of regret. It wasn't just lust between them; it couldn't be. Yet it couldn't be anything else.

Once more he leaned down and brushed her lips, then arranged his body so that he could continue to hold her. They didn't speak; he was sure that neither of them would know what to say. Content merely to be close, they held each other as they flew through the night back to their hotel.

Back to their past.

Back to thwarted desire.

And it was growing closer to midnight.

NINE

A sleepy Erica leaned against Conner as he inserted the key card into the door lock of their suite. Her eyes were closed. She looked as if she were still as caught up in the drive home from the party as he was.

Conner opened the door and sent up a silent prayer that the hotel had had enough time to move him and Erica back in and follow the rest of his instructions.

"Are we staying in our suite, Conner?"

"Yes."

"Do we still have a guard?"

"No. I've released him for now." Conner glanced into the parlor. "Don't open your eyes," he instructed.

"But I can't see where I'm going."

"That's all right, I'll direct you."

Placing both hands on her shoulders, Conner

walked Erica through the door, across the parlor, and into her room.

"Why don't you get out of your party dress and into something more comfortable? I have a surprise for you."

"All right." Erica felt too warm and happy to disagree with anything.

Moments later she was wearing her favorite sleep shirt with the teddy bear on the front. She tugged on a pair of clean socks and slipped her arms into the hotel robe.

"May I come out now?"

"If you close your eyes again." Conner was outside her door instantly, opening it, taking her hand and tugging her eagerly into the parlor. "Now," he said, "open them."

In the center of the parlor was a live green tree surrounded by boxes of Christmas decorations and strands of lights.

"A Christmas tree?"

"Your Christmas tree," Conner said.

"Oh, Conner, it's beautiful. How did you do it?" She plopped down on the floor beside the boxes and looked up at the tree, her eyes glistening with moisture.

"I find things, remember." Or, rather, he thought, Sterling does. He'd give her another raise tomorrow. She'd turn it down just like she had the last three. She already had everything she wanted, she always said.

Erica was tearing the boxes open, admiring the decorations.

"Do you want to decorate it tonight?" he asked. "Or would you rather wait until tomorrow?"

Erica sprang to her feet and drew Conner over to the tree. "Tomorrow? Are you kidding? I want to decorate it right now. What do we do first?"

Conner had to smile. Suddenly it was ten years ago and they were rediscovering the delight of sharing something new. It had been a lot of years since he'd decorated a tree. In fact, the last one had been a pine branch on a ratty piece of real estate in a country that didn't even celebrate Christmas. "The lights, I think."

Moments later Erica had shed her robe and had a rope of twinkling lights spread across her legs. "They all work, Conner. I'll hand the strand to you and you wind it around the tree."

With a few alterations of location, a couple of tangled arms, and not so secret touches, they got the lights on the tree. Next came the ornaments. Conner looked at the ceramic Santas and the silver bells and decided the simple red and green balls he remembered from childhood had come a long way.

He managed to keep his hands off Erica and his mind away from making love to her until she dropped her ornament and leaned over to pick it up. Her nightshirt was long, but not long enough to cover the lacy panties beneath.

"Ah, hell!" He swore and tightened his grip on

his bell. Moments later it was crushed in his hand, the jagged edges digging into his palm.

"Conner, you're hurt!" Erica rushed into the bathroom and brought back a wet hand towel. Drawing him to the light, she brushed the pieces of glass into the waste can, examining the wound until she was certain it was clear. "Wait right here. There's a first aid kit in my room."

"I'm fine, Erica. Really, I am."

But his Dragon Lady was having no part of that. This was something she could do for Conner and do it she would. After applying the ointment and stretching a gauze bandage around his hand, she leaned back and looked up at him, a worried expression on her face.

"Does it hurt?"

"No. It's okay. But I think I prefer the old kiss-it-and-make-it-better method of treatment."

Her eyes widened. Her breathing slowed. "I—I can do that, but we have to put the star on the tree first."

"Yes," he said, releasing her for just a second to reach down and pick up the silvery tree topper and thread it over the center branch at the top. He shoved the plug into the nearest strand of lights and the star burst into a radiant shower of gold.

"Oh, Conner," Erica whispered, "it's beautiful. Nobody ever did anything like this for me before. Thank you."

Conner glanced at the bandage on his hand, catching sight of his watch.

It was midnight.

She held perfectly still. And then he kissed her, fleetingly at first, leaving her stunned and wanting more. Her heart hammered beneath the worn cotton of her shirt. After so many years of trying to close out the devastating power of his touch, she was about to know it again, in the most intimate way. What had happened in the past was best left there. Both had been guilty of assuming the worst of the other. Her plan to punish him for his abandonment vanished with his kiss.

"You are so beautiful," he murmured huskily. "I've wanted you, this, us for so long. I just wouldn't let myself face it." His teeth nipped at her ear while his good hand skimmed her hips and pulled her against him.

Conner seemed to be in no hurry. She laid her forehead on his shoulder, allowing a sigh to escape. Her heart was beating erratically, as was his. She could feel his arousal pulsating against her, feel his body quivering with need.

He leaned back until haunted dark eyes met stormy blue ones. "You know I want to make love with you."

Her breath caught in her throat. She could only nod.

His injured hand continued to hold her while the other one moved beneath her arm and cupped her breast, pausing to hold it for a long time before finding the tight bud of her nipple. "God knows,

I've tried to forget you, but there's never been another woman for me."

Erica arched back, pushing her breast into his hand. Her nipples were deliciously sensitive, peaking with desire, every bit as aroused as the hard evidence of his need pressed against her.

"Talk to me, Erica. Don't let me do this alone."

Dazed, she tried to respond, but the words wouldn't come. She moistened her lips and finally managed to say, "Conner."

"Say it again," he demanded in a ragged voice. His lips claimed the spot where her pulse was flaring in the hollow of her throat. Moving downward, his fingers caressed her bare stomach as he bunched the material of her shirt between them. The maddeningly slow caresses made her writhe beneath his touch.

"Conner, wait." With one little movement she slipped the shirt from her body. Wearing only lacy panties and her socks, she wanted to feel his bare skin against hers. Unbuttoning his shirt, she slid it from his shoulders to the floor. His belt and trousers soon followed. He'd already shed his shoes and socks. There was no mistaking the degree of his desire. She couldn't bring herself to go any further.

"Why'd you stop?" he asked, hooking his thumbs beneath the waistband of his briefs and tugging them down. His lips stopped at her belly button, tasting, caressing as he lifted her feet and removed her socks. She sighed in pleasure as he moved his attention to the only piece of clothing that came between them. He slowly peeled away the wisps of lace, leaving her completely nude.

Suddenly shy, she put her hands on his shoulders and closed the distance between them, whimpering as the tips of her nipples grazed his chest in delicious torture.

He drew her arms behind his neck and backed up until he reached the sofa. Leaning against it, he cupped her bottom with his hands and lifted her, laying that throbbing part of him against the moist wetness of her desire in tender torment.

With eyes closed, he moved up and down, almost plunging inside her, then sliding away. He could feel her heart beating, merging wildly with his own. A firestorm of sensation was building.

"We shouldn't be doing this," he managed to say.

She gasped. "Do you want to stop?"

"No! I don't ever want to stop."

"Now, Conner. Now!"

But he didn't take her. Instead, he slid across her in slow, drugging thrusts. His mouth captured her lips again, his tongue picking up the pace his body had slowed. In tantalizing her beyond all reason, he was driving himself to the point of internal combustion.

Then, when he felt her frantic moans, he turned and laid her on the couch, one knee wedged between her thighs, supporting his weight by keeping his other foot on the floor.

Poised over her, Conner stared down at her. "You know there is no going back now, darling."

Erica whispered yes. She knew. Reaching up, she pulled his mouth down to hers and kissed him with all the need inside her. She was agonizingly aware of his body, his size and heat, his hesitation. When she could endure it no more, she slipped her hands down his back and pressed him down, rising to meet him.

As he entered her she gave a cry of pleasure, hugging his thighs with her own. Her blood began to roar. She rocked wildly, tugging her lips away. "Now, Conner. Together!"

Above her, his face contorted with desire so intense that he appeared to be in pain. As her own release ripped through her, she felt the clench of his body, then the hot heat of his pleasure filled her.

They were both still vibrating as he fell against her, planting his face in the nape of her neck, holding her hands over her head as if he were afraid she'd manage to slip away.

Beneath him, she felt warm and weak and safe.

The lights of the Christmas tree threw muted colors against the ceiling. She had the feeling that they were in the center of a kaleidoscope; any movement changed the pattern of light into another beautiful array of color.

For a long time they lay, still joined, each breathing evenly, acutely aware of the other. Finally Conner moved to the side, pulling her close. She wanted to remain like this forever. For now she nestled against him, cherishing the moment, gathering memories to last forever.

The pressure of his lips against her hair said that he too was caught up in the afterglow of their lovemaking. She sighed and snuggled closer.

Beside her, Conner was gripped by such a feeling of pure contentment that he couldn't speak. He'd been sexually satisfied before. But this was something new.

Her breast grazed his chest with every breath she took. The splendor of the moment still washed over him in diminishing waves of pleasure.

After a delicious moment, he felt Erica move her head. "Conner?"

Here it comes, he thought, the regret, the good bye.

"My bottom is getting cold. I think I'm ready for bed."

Conner bit back a sigh of dismay. He came to his feet and helped her to rise. Reluctant to let her go, he pulled her close and kissed her. Then he picked her up and carried her to her room. Pulling back the covers, he helped her into the bed, then covered her.

"Where are you going?" she asked sleepily.

"I thought . . ."

"Don't think, Conner." She pulled back the cover and smiled.

He didn't need a second invitation.

They made love twice more during the night, each time more beautiful than the time before. By the time Erica opened her eyes the next morning, the sun was high in the sky. Sleepily she reached out, expecting to find Conner's bare body beside her.

It wasn't.

There was only her neatly folded robe lying across the foot of the bed. Alarmed, she sat up and looked around. She was definitely alone. The cover was pulled up beside her as if nobody had ever been there. A cold ripple of fear swept over her. Had she dreamed it all?

Pulling on the robe, Erica wandered into the parlor, where the Christmas tree they'd decorated so lovingly still twinkled. No, it couldn't have been a dream. Here was the proof, that and the soreness of her body.

But where was he?

Then she saw the note, propped against a breakfast tray on the table.

> *My darling Erica. You are so beautiful sleeping beside me. I don't want to leave you, but I have an errand I must run. Eat breakfast and think of me. I'll be back soon.*
>
> *Conner*

Erica drew the notepaper to her lips, imagining that they were touching Conner's. Then she lifted the warmer from the platter and smiled.

Chocolate muffins.

Drinking her coffee and eating the muffins, she wondered what kind of errand he could possibly have on Christmas Eve day. When the last of the crumbs were gone and the coffeepot was empty, she wandered about the suite, just touching and remembering. In Conner's room she lay down on his tightly made bed, reveling in the wrinkles she was leaving behind.

The Conner she'd known ten years ago had been anything but neat. It had been Erica who'd folded and put away their clothes, straightened the newspapers and brushed away the crumbs Conner had scattered about their bed. Now it was hard to tell that Conner occupied the room. Only the remaining drops of water in the shower and the crumpled towel thrown across the tub gave evidence of his presence.

Clasping her arms around herself, Erica took in a deep, satisfied breath. A cool, refreshing scent filled the air. She opened the containers on the counter until she found its source, a bottle of aftershave called simply Sky. Its blue bottle and fresh smell was definitely Conner.

Erica caught sight of herself in the mirror and gasped. Her cheeks and neck were rosy, a result of Conner's five o'clock shadow, no doubt. Her lips were swollen and pouty from the hard, demanding kisses she'd shared. Everything about her proclaimed that she was a woman who'd been thoroughly loved.

She blushed and wondered what Conner would think if he came back and found her looking all misty-eyed in his mirror. With that thought, a sense of lonely uncertainty settled over her. Where was Conner and why had he left her?

A shower, here in Conner's bathroom, using Conner's things, offered the return of the closeness they'd shared the night before.

Minutes later she'd lathered soap over her body and felt the stinging hot water wash away the scent of their lovemaking, replacing it with the clean smell of Conner, the man. She shampooed her hair, lingering in the shower as if it might keep him close. Finally, she reached for the rumpled towel, still damp from drying his body, and rubbed herself dry.

Back in her room, she dressed in a pair of dark slacks and a bright red sweater. The sweater was as seasonal as she could get on Christmas. What she needed—what they needed—were presents under the tree. As soon as Conner returned, they'd go shopping—unless . . . of course, that's where he was, buying Christmas presents.

Tempted to do the same, she started toward the door. Then she remembered the last time she had done such a thing, and stopped. When Conner returned, she'd convince him to take her shopping.

But what to do until then?

She wandered back and forth, turning on the TV, then turning it off again. Finally she went to her desk. She'd call Mac and check on the ambassador. But the line was busy.

She paced back and forth, contemplating what she'd learned last night at Brighton Kilgore's party. She knew nothing more about Brighton except that he'd worked for the government at one time as an inspector of some kind.

It was Karl Ernst who worried her. He had asked about the ambassador's location and denied that he'd known about the piece of broken marble she and Bart had found. Then there was his story about Bart being afraid that he was being followed. Why would Bart ask about an American student breaking the law if it wasn't about the piece of marble?

Why would Bart think he was being followed, and if he were, who would have done it? Had Bart gone to the embassy as Mr. Ernst had suggested?

Too many questions with no answers.

Where was Conner?

Erica tried to reach Shangrila again. This time she got the recording which asked her to identify herself and someone would return her call. She gave her name and number and hung up.

Where was Mac? Why didn't he answer her call? She'd never called and reached the answering machine before. She was beginning to have a bad feeling.

Conner Preston. Erica Fallon. Without realizing she'd done so, Erica had written their names on the notepad by the phone and drawn a heart around them. She dropped the pen as if it were burning her hand.

When the phone finally rang she nearly jumped out of her skin. "Hello?"

"Erica," the ambassador's familiar voice said. "Good, I'm glad I reached you. I need to see you right away."

"You want me to fly back there?"

"Not necessary. I'm in New Orleans."

"You're here? Are you all right?"

"I'm tired, but I'm recovering."

Erica's mind raced. She picked up the pen, ready to take directions. *The ambassador in New Orleans?* She added a series of question marks. What had happened to bring him here? "Where are you?"

"I'm in the lobby. Can you come down?"

"Of course." Erica grabbed her purse and jacket and flew out the door. So she didn't have a return elevator key. She'd leave a message at the desk for Conner. He'd come for her.

As she stepped off the elevator, two men moved up beside her. One was a stranger. The second man she recognized from Brighton's dinner party—his secretary, Mr. Boykin. "Act natural," he said in that familiar southern voice. "We may be watched."

Erica suddenly remembered where she'd heard that voice before—on the street when she'd been pushed. "Where is the ambassador?" Erica asked.

"He's in the limo outside."

"Just a minute," she said, hesitating. "I need to leave a message for—"

"No time!" Boykin said.

Erica jerked away. "I don't know what you think you're doing, but I know you're the one who pushed me. Let me go or I'll scream!"

"And if you do, the ambassador will die. Just look through the doors to the limo."

She followed his instructions and caught sight of the ambassador's worried face through the open glass. He attempted a smile, then glanced to the seat in front as if he were telling her that someone was there.

Erica had walked into a trap, just like Conner and Bart. She shivered, hoping that the result wouldn't be the same. *Conner, if you have ever had me watched, I hope it's now.* Erica gave one quick look behind her. No one seemed remotely interested in what was happening to her. So be it, she thought. *I'm the one who caused all this to begin with, it's up to me to end it.*

Her companions closed in and walked her toward the doors, one in front and one behind.

"Miss Fallon?" One of the doormen started toward her. "Is everything all right?"

"Get rid of him," Boykin growled.

"Yes, thanks," she replied as her companion casually pushed her into the revolving glass door and out onto the sidewalk beyond.

The limo door opened and she was thrust inside to the vacant seat opposite the wounded diplomat.

"You shouldn't have come, Ambassador."

"Once I heard you were in New Orleans with Preston, I had to come. I couldn't let it go any further. But these men were waiting when I stepped off the plane."

At that moment Boykin closed the passenger door and slid into the front seat, opening the glass partition between.

"Enjoy the ride," Boykin said. "You have plenty of time to decide what you're going to do before we get where we're going."

"And where is that?" the ambassador demanded in a thready voice.

"Just shut up, old man. Don't make me give you another bullet wound."

Erica's question slipped out before she could hold it back. "You're the one who shot him in New York?"

"No, but I'll be the one who shoots him here."

The ambassador shook his head. "Don't do anything foolish, Erica."

Erica looked around, studying the interior of the limo. She had to figure a way to alert someone to their plight.

"Conner Preston will come after you," she warned, searching for a way to distract Boykin. Maybe the door . . .

"Don't even think it," he warned. "The panel up here overrides all the controls back there. Just be sensible and stay calm. Have something to drink."

"No thanks," Erica shot back, then remembered the ambassador. "Unless you'd like something, sir?" Solicitously, she leaned forward, taking in the pallor of the man she'd served for the last nine years. She'd learned early on that he wasn't a strong man, physically or mentally. Bolstering him up was one of the duties she'd taken on.

"No—nothing, Erica. Just do what he says."

"And if I don't?"

"I'll kill him," the southern voice said, "then I'll get the boyfriend."

"No. Don't hurt Ambassador Collins."

The ambassador seemed to collect himself and leaned forward. "I won't sit here and let anyone be hurt."

"Don't worry, sir," Erica reassured him. "I'm sure that Conner will come for us."

The ambassador gave her an odd smile. "Sometimes, my dear, the best laid plans fall apart."

Conner, sitting at the bar in the Napoleon House, glanced at his watch for the dozenth time. He'd been waiting for more than an hour. It was obvious that his informant wasn't coming. Throwing a couple of bills on the counter, Conner left the restaurant and started back to the hotel.

It had taken all the fortitude he possessed to make himself leave Erica that morning. He'd ordered coffee and muffins, then showered, resolved that Erica should get some rest after their night of lovemaking. When the phone had rung, he'd assumed it would be Mac or Sterling, either of whom would be soundly rewarded if they accomplished what he hadn't allowed himself to do—wake Erica.

The caller was neither. The voice was low and unidentifiable. "Mr. Preston, I have information about your brother's death. Are you interested?"

"Who is this?"

"Doesn't matter. It's what I have to say that you'll want to hear."

"Say it."

"Not on the phone. Come to the Napoleon House. Wait at the bar for further instructions."

"Give me half an hour."

"You have fifteen minutes."

The phone went dead and Conner was left with no choice but to follow the order he'd been given. Behind him, Erica was still sleeping. He toyed with waking her, then decided to leave a note. Pushing his time limit, he scrawled a second note, dropped it and the snapshots of the statue into an envelope addressed to Mac, and tossed it at the desk clerk to be mailed as he jogged past.

Now Conner glanced at his watch. He'd been gone too long. Christmas Eve, he thought, eyeing the tourists moving through the Quarter. He wondered if Erica was up yet. What would she think when she found herself alone?

Alone!

Damn! He'd been set up—again. It was so obvious, even a schoolboy would have seen it. He would have seen it, too, if he hadn't spent most of the night making love to Erica. If his mind hadn't been so filled with her.

Love?

Yes, dammit. Love. He'd been crazy in love with her ten years ago when he'd walked straight into an ambush and he was still in love with her. He'd never stopped loving her. And she felt the same about him. Or she had, until now. Whoever called him had wanted him away from the hotel.

From Erica.

Conner broke into a run, brushing aside the people who were in his way, feeling his heart slam against his lungs. In the lobby, he ran past the doorman and into the elevator, ignoring the voice calling out to him from behind. The parlor was unoccupied, though he could see where Erica had drunk coffee and eaten a muffin.

And the bedroom was empty. No Erica. Her jacket and purse were gone. His eyes covered the area, zeroing in on the notepad. He saw their names, surrounded by the heart. Then *The ambassador—in New Orleans???* Damn! They'd gotten to her in the only way she wouldn't have suspected. "Where are you, Erica?"

There was a knock at the door. Conner opened it.

"Mr. Preston?" It was the doorman.

"If you're looking for Miss Fallon, I saw her in the lobby with two men earlier. I called out to her, but she assured me that she was okay. Should I have stopped her?"

"Yes, but you couldn't have known. Tell me about the men."

The doorman described the two kidnappers, but nothing he said helped identify them until he got to the soft-spoken man with a southern accent.

Kilgore's secretary. "Where did they go?" Conner asked.

"They got into a limo and drove away."

"Anything else you can think of? Anything at all?"

"Only that there was a man inside the limo."

"Tall, blondish, thin?" Brighton Kilgore, Conner was thinking.

"No. Tall maybe, but his hair was almost gray. And he looked ill."

The ambassador? That made no sense. If the ambassador had left Shangrila, Mac would have told him. Unless something had happened to Mac. Conner turned back to the elevator. He needed to consider every possibility. This was no search and rescue operation that he'd spent months planning. This was Erica, who still loved him. He couldn't afford any mistakes.

Yesterday he might have wondered if she was setting a trap for him, an elaborate trap that had been planned down to the minute, including the note with their names written in a heart. Today he didn't give the idea a second thought.

"Don't guess you got a license number, did you?"

"No, but I believe it was the same limo that

came for you last evening. There aren't many made by that manufacturer in New Orleans."

"Thanks," Conner said, turning back inside.

"Shall I call the police, sir?"

"No. No, not yet."

Conner moved back to Erica's desk, where he discovered the red message button pulsating. He studied Erica's note until the operator came back on the line.

"A Mr. MacAllister returned Ms. Fallon's call," she said. "He says it's urgent that he reach either Mr. Preston or Ms. Fallon. His number is—"

"Never mind," Conner interrupted, disconnected the operator, and punched in the numbers.

"Lincoln MacAllister here."

"Mac, Conner. Erica's missing."

"So is the ambassador," Mac said.

"How did he get away from your stronghold?"

"He talked to Brighton Kilgore and learned that you and Erica were in New Orleans. Then he suddenly packed his clothes and demanded that he be flown there."

"So, she was right. He is here. Is he well enough to travel?"

"Technically, yes. But he's very weak and worried. What have you learned?"

"The night before the wedding Bart thought he was being followed. He may have gone to the embassy for protection. Is there any way you can check that?"

"Hmm. Don't know. I'll check the log. Didn't he say anything to you?"

"He tried. But I was celebrating and I put him off."

"I'll get back to you," Mac promised. "What's your next move?"

"I'm going to see Kilgore," Conner answered.

"What do you want from him?"

"Information. I suspect that he's already providing southern hospitality to a very diverse Christmas gathering."

"What are you going to do?"

Conner gave a strained, "Ho! Ho! Ho! I'm going to play Santa Claus."

TEN

Erica refused to be intimidated by the sly smile of William Boykin, who was watching them through the open glass partition. The more she saw of him, the more like a weasel he became.

"If you want my cooperation," she snapped, "you'll allow me to talk to the ambassador in private."

"As long as we get what we want, you can have whatever you like, princess," Boykin agreed.

A moment later an opaque glass slid down between the two compartments and Erica and the ambassador were alone. She located the intercom and turned it off, though after Boykin's comment about the control panel, she couldn't be certain that their conversation was blocked.

"Are you really all right, sir?"

"A bit weak, but I'm getting stronger."

He might say he was recovering, but Erica could

see the strain in his face. "What made you decide to come here?"

"I was worried about you. I couldn't hide out inside some mountain while you're risking your life. What have you and Preston learned?"

Erica could have told him about being pushed on the sidewalk and about their suite being searched, but there was no point in worrying him more. "So far, nothing. The only thing I'm certain of is that one of our kidnappers is Brighton Kilgore's secretary, William Boykin."

The ambassador was clearly surprised. "Kilgore's secretary?"

"Do you think Mr. Kilgore is behind all this? Didn't we have security reports run on the committee?"

"The report that came to me said he was a successful businessman and an avid art collector. There was no suggestion that he was engaged in anything illegal."

"Then why is this happening?"

"Erica, I hate to say this, but I'm beginning to wonder if our benefactor, Mr. MacAllister, might be involved in it somehow. How else could these men know I was coming and be waiting for me when I stepped off the plane?"

That question stopped her for a moment. Conner had been rescued by Mac. Mac had been the one to investigate what had happened ten years ago and the ambassador had been in Mac's care. "No."

She shook her head. "I don't believe that for a moment."

"Neither do I, really," the ambassador admitted. "From the beginning it's been the book, Erica. They expect me to convince you to turn it over to them."

"But I don't have it, I don't even know what it is." Erica said. "And I wouldn't give it to them if I did."

"Of course not. But if the committee could get hold of it, maybe we could make some sense of what's happening here."

"It's all so hopeless," she said. "I don't believe it exists."

Ambassador Collins shot a worried look over his shoulder at the men up front, then slipped across to the seat next to Erica. He leaned close and said in a low whisper, "I think it might exist, Erica. I know Bart had some secret he was hiding."

Erica felt her gut clench. "A secret?"

"Yes. The night before you and Preston were to be married, Bart came to the embassy. He believed that someone was following him, asked all kinds of questions about what happened to Americans who broke German law. He seemed worried."

"Why didn't you say anything before?"

"I was just a junior staff member at the time, and the situation in West Berlin was volatile. Then Bart was killed and I didn't know what to do. I didn't want to make trouble for the boy. I tried to reach Preston, but he'd been sent back to the States.

Then I was sent to Paris and I let it slide. Now I've put you in danger."

Ambassador Collins let out a weary sigh, leaned his head against the seat back, and closed his eyes. He looked so pale. Maybe a drink would help. She quickly located a bottle of wine in the little bar and filled a glass for the ambassador.

"Here, drink this." She forced the glass into his hand. "It will make you feel better."

"No." He pushed it away. "I'll be fine. Really I will. I just need to rest for a moment. You drink it."

Erica looked around helplessly. Somehow, possibly because of her, the man who'd come to her rescue ten years ago had been shot. She took a swallow of wine and said a silent prayer that Conner knew where they were.

She glanced at the partition separating them from their kidnappers, drained the glass, and under the cover of returning the bar to its proper position searched for a phone. There wasn't one.

"Please," she said, trying unsuccessfully to lower the side window. "You mustn't hold yourself responsible. We simply have to find a way to convince them there is no book."

"I don't believe they'll accept that, Erica. Think. Think hard. Don't you ever remember Bart keeping a diary?"

"Never. What do they think the book is supposed to reveal?"

The ambassador sat up and took Erica's hand. "I've been pondering that. What if Bart found something valuable, something he documented. But if he had, you'd know about that, wouldn't you?"

"Of course I would. He and I were partners. If Bart had—" But then she stopped. During the last weeks she hadn't been with Bart. She'd fallen in love with Conner and nothing else had mattered.

Erica suddenly felt as if thousands of spiders were crawling over her skin. The truth was, she didn't know. She drew in a raspy breath, facing the final truth.

"No, at the end I was with Conner. Bart continued his research alone. I knew he was working hard, but if he discovered something, he never told me."

"What about Preston?" Ambassador Collins asked. "When Bart left my office that night, he was going to talk with his brother. Did you see Bart the night before the wedding?"

"Yes. He came to my apartment, but when he learned that Conner had already gone back to the base, he left. He said he had something to do the next morning and he'd see me at the church. I never saw Bart again."

"When those men kidnapped you and took your notes and Bart's portfolio, there was no book or you would have seen it." He cut his eyes in her direction. "And you didn't."

"No. But if it was a private diary, it could have been there and I wouldn't have recognized it for what it was."

"Maybe."

Clearly her employer was skeptical. "Why, after

all these years, are people suddenly looking for this book?"

"Because of Kilgore's statue. It was listed as one of the stolen pieces and suddenly it turns up."

The night before still weighed heavily on Erica's mind. "Why do you suppose Kilgore showed us the statue? If it was stolen, wouldn't he want that kept quiet?"

"He and Ernst thought it might draw out the thief. If he thought he could sell others with no reprisal, the culprit might contact Kilgore."

"So why doesn't Mr. Kilgore tell the committee where the statue came from? Then we'll know who has the book."

The ambassador glanced uneasily at the divider, then checked the intercom again to make certain it was off. "We know where he got it. That soldier of fortune he hired located it for him—the man called Shadow."

Erica couldn't help letting out a sound of disbelief. "A soldier of fortune? I don't believe it. And where did this man called Shadow get it?"

"This isn't the first piece that has turned up. It's just the first one we've been able to trace. According to Brighton, Shadow located the statue and offered it to him. When it turned out to be authentic, Ernst figured that somebody, maybe Bart's brother, maybe you, gave Bart's diary to Shadow."

Erica was stunned. They actually thought that she or Conner had Bart's book and therefore the treasure. "Then why not kidnap Conner?"

The ambassador pursed his lips in thought before finally answering. "Conner is a powerful man with powerful friends. Perhaps they needed some kind of leverage to force him to cooperate. You provided it."

Erica was beginning to feel very tired. It was becoming hard to concentrate. "I don't understand."

"Since you and Conner are together again, they're going to hold you hostage until they get what they want."

"But they've kidnapped you too. Why?"

"I suppose they think I know too much."

"So they're going to swap me for Bart's book?" Erica didn't know whether to laugh or let the ambassador know she was scared to death. "Well, I know Conner Preston, and he isn't going to deal with criminals. They've made a big mistake."

"I hope you're wrong, Erica. I'm old. I don't matter anymore, but you're the daughter I never had. I don't want you to be hurt."

She was touched. This man who'd taken her in had risked his own life to protect her. Now, he'd placed himself in danger again. "Don't be silly. Conner will find us."

The ambassador patted Erica's arm in what was meant to be a reassuring gesture but seemed instead to border on desperation. "Once the book is produced, they'll let you—us go."

"And what will happen then?" Erica was suddenly suspicious of the lack of interest shown by Boykin and the driver.

"The committee will discover where the treasures are stored. Mr. Ernst claims the art for Germany, who will return it to its rightful owners and Brighton collects a portion of the artwork as his finder's fee. And maybe, after this is all over, I'll get a new post as my reward for finding the treasure."

Erica didn't have the heart to tell her employer that no matter the outcome, she didn't believe he'd get a post of any importance. None of this would have happened if she and Conner hadn't decided to use their relationship as a ploy to reach the criminals. No, she corrected herself, Conner had come up with the plan to force her attacker's hand. She had to get to Conner and ask him about Shadow's part in the sale of the statue. Conner would tell her the truth. Conner didn't lie.

Outside the limo, the sky was growing darker. The impending bad weather seemed at hand. There'd be no bonfires welcoming Santa tonight. A sudden slash of water against the window announced the arrival of the rain.

Her eyelids grew heavy. She could hardly keep them open. What was happening? Erica gazed at Ambassador Collins in bewilderment. There was a humming in her ears that grew louder. Then she understood. Her blurred vision was not from confusion or lack of sleep. The wine had been drugged. As she slid into darkness she heard herself protesting, "They're wrong about all this. There is no book."

Shadow was in his element. Clad in black from his black boots to his ski mask, he turned the rental car down Kilgore's drive. If he'd been able to set his time, he would have waited for night, but he was afraid to delay. Whoever was behind Erica's abduction had made the choice.

The day had turned dark and gray with a fine mist blowing in from the river. Now the storm was arriving in full force. Thick, heavy clouds hung low, as if they were reaching for the ground. Long ago he'd learned to make use of whatever he was provided with. He'd use the storm.

Conner parked the car. Slipping through the trees toward the castle in the middle of the afternoon on Christmas Eve day was not what he'd envisioned when he'd arranged for Erica's Christmas tree. He cursed himself for not protecting her better.

When he'd learned what happened, Conner's usual icy demeanor had deserted him. All he could think about was Erica. They'd warned her three times, now they'd acted. And he'd let it happen.

He should have been ready. This wasn't the first kidnapping, nor was it the first demand for information. Erica had claimed that she missed their wedding because she'd been taken by Green Berets who were searching for the reference material she and Bart had compiled for their project. Could Bart have made other notes without her knowledge?

In retrospect, Conner regretted neglecting Bart. Once he and Erica had fallen in love, nothing else in their lives had been important. He'd convinced Erica to leave their project to Bart. Over Bart's objections she'd ignored her studies and research and spent all her time with Conner. He hated to admit it, but looking back, Bart had been preoccupied. He'd tried to talk to Conner, the night before the ceremony, but Conner had been out celebrating with his unit and put Bart off until after the wedding.

Then there had been no wedding.

Behind him, thunder rolled across the river. The storm was almost over them. The lights inside the castle were coming on. A sharp bolt of lightning split the sky, forcing Conner to duck behind the magnolia tree.

The mist turned into rain as he slid from one tree to the next, and Conner felt his adrenaline flare. From the sophisticated persona of Conner Preston, he became the man who could walk through a room filled with people and not be seen.

This was where he excelled. Impossible missions had been his specialty as a Green Beret. In the military he'd learned to go anywhere. He became a legend. Afterward, he'd continued to hone his skills. Stopping for a moment, he took in a slow, measured breath.

Conner was gone. Shadow was here.

Moments later Shadow spotted the limo. At the rear of the house he looked through the kitchen window and saw Mrs. Kilgore in deep conversation with a woman he decided was the cook. Soundlessly, he moved toward the door, feeling the intensity of white-hot anger that told him he was right.

The back door was unlocked. In a moment he was inside the service entrance, and when the cook followed Mrs. Kilgore into another room, Shadow found the castle's power box. Another second and he'd disabled the electricity and the castle plunged into darkness.

He gave his eyes a moment to adjust to the darkness. Now, where to start? They—whoever "they" were—wouldn't hold Erica in an area that was too accessible.

If Erica was in the castle, Brighton Kilgore had to be involved. The ambassador's name doodled on the notepad along with the possibility of his presence was still a puzzle. Nothing made sense.

But there was no doubt in his mind that all this was a ruse designed to force someone, either Conner Preston or Shadow, to do what they'd been unable to do.

Find the book.

Keeping a sharp ear to pinpoint the location of Kilgore's guests, Shadow was able to avoid them. With cautious use of his pocket flashlight, he made his way through the castle, from one room to another, searching, studying the layout of the structure. Finally, only two places remained unexamined: the locked gallery and the basement, or, as Brighton had referred to it, the dungeon.

He glanced at the luminous hand on his watch. Five o'clock. Time was running out. The basement, then the gallery. He headed back toward the servants' quarters and the steps that led down. There were several voices arguing about the cause of the power failure. He heard Mrs. Kilgore send Boykin for her husband while Joseph checked the fuse box.

Oblivious of danger, Boykin dashed past Shadow and down the steps. Shadow moved silently behind Kilgore's secretary.

With his fingertips grazing the damp walls, Shadow was able to penetrate the absolute darkness in silence. He paused when he heard a door open at the end of the corridor.

"Mr. Kilgore," Boykin began.

"What the hell's happening up there?" Kilgore bellowed.

"Power's out," Boykin answered. "Must be the storm. Joseph's working on it."

As the men inside talked, Shadow felt the tingling sense of danger that always intensified when he was close to his target.

His cloak of fear, he called it. That added kick of intensity that made him invincible. It felt good. For the past ten years he'd felt alive only when he pushed himself to this point and beyond—until Erica had come back into his life.

"Are you sure it isn't Shadow?" Erica asked. "You wanted him. This is his kind of danger."

She was here. *Careful, Dragon Lady, they're pretty edgy.*

Though he didn't need it to see, he flicked on his flashlight, gave the door a shove, and stepped into the room. The man behind the door went down in a clatter.

Immediately the conversation stopped, the occupants of the room staring like wild animals frozen in fear. All they could see was the outline of a man dressed in black, a gun in one hand and a flashlight in the other.

"Shadow!" Erica whispered. Like a scene in a B movie, she'd been tied to a chair. "You're actually here."

Shadow felt their fear. He flicked his light on the man he'd knocked down. "Hello, Kilgore. Sorry, didn't mean to soil your trousers." He turned back to the older man. "You must be Ambassador Collins. How are you, sir?"

"A little weak," the man answered in a shaky voice. "These men kidnapped Erica and me. Thank God you've come."

"We're all here, aren't we," Shadow said. "Everybody except Ernst. Somebody went to a lot of trouble to arrange that. I'd like to know who. Do you know anything about this, Ambassador?"

"Certainly not. You really don't think I had any part in this, do you?" Ambassador Collins's voice was so tight now, he could hardly speak. "Erica? I came here to take care of you."

"I know," she answered. "This is silly, Shadow.

The ambassador has been like a father to me. He took me in when I was released from the hospital. I wouldn't have made it without him."

Conner shot a sharp glance at Erica. That was the second time he'd heard about an illness. Had Erica been hurt somehow and her condition concealed?

He badly wanted to touch her, to tell her that everything was going to be okay, but there was no time now. Kilgore was slowly edging his way toward the door.

"I wouldn't do that, Kilgore," Shadow threatened, swinging his light to the man. "I'm ready to listen to what you have to say, unless you'd rather explain this to the police."

Kilgore flinched. "No—no police. The publicity would completely ruin me."

Shadow's light didn't waver. "Why'd you have the ambassador shot? He could have died—like Bart."

Kilgore began to babble. "He wasn't supposed to be hurt. Nobody was. It was meant to be a warning. We just wanted the book and we had to make sure you understood that. If we get—"

"Once and for all," Erica interrupted. "He doesn't have the book."

"Suppose you got the book," Shadow offered almost in a whisper. "What then?"

"I think I can answer that," the ambassador said. "With the book, they'd learn Bart's secret. They believe he found the location of the hidden art treasures."

"So this is all about greed," Conner said.

"Of course not," Kilgore spoke up. "Restoration of the stolen treasures. We'd have the undying gratitude of the United Nations and all the countries who lost their art."

Shadow rocked back and forth on the balls of his feet. "Pure altruism," he drawled. "I don't think I believe that. What's in it for you and Mr. Ernst?"

"Well," Kilgore admitted, "we figured that there would be a finder's fee. I'd claim that—in treasure. And Ernst would finally gain respect and prestige for returning the treasures."

"Something for everyone," Shadow said softly.

"Stop stalling," Kilgore said. "You promised the book. Where is it?"

"Believe me, gentlemen," Shadow replied. "I would give it to you if I had it. But I don't—not yet. Now, untie Ms. Fallon. We're leaving."

"I don't think so," a familiar voice said.

Karl Ernst stepped inside the room, coming to a stop behind Conner.

"This is a gun you feel against your backbone," Ernst threatened.

"Finally, the last Musketeer," Shadow said. "I wondered when you'd show up."

Erica felt the undercurrent of fear in the room. Brighton Kilgore was no match for Shadow, but Karl Ernst was another story. She began to struggle.

The ambassador cleared his throat. "Stop this. I won't have Erica hurt."

"And she won't be," Karl promised, "if she and her rescuer cooperate. All we—I want is to locate the treasures. And one way or another, I intend to have it, even if I have to kill all of you."

"That would be foolish, wouldn't it?" Shadow asked. "Without us you'll be back where you were when you killed Bart."

"We thought we had his records. All we had to do was silence Bart and Ms. Fallon."

"Bart died because of your greed. Be glad I'm here," Shadow said, "instead of Preston. He'd tear your head off."

Ernst wasn't going to be swayed. "The book, I'll take it now." He moved toward Erica's side.

"Drop your gun, Shadow, unless you need another warning."

Ernst pointed his weapon directly at Erica, its shiny finish reflecting the light and underscoring the menace.

Shadow flipped on the safety and dropped the Beretta.

Erica struggled to free herself.

"You knew then, didn't you, Ernst?" Conner asked. "You knew that Bart had found something. That's why the men you hired demanded Erica's notes and Bart's portfolio. You thought they'd tell you what you wanted. And you killed Bart?"

"He wasn't supposed to die."

Shadow drew on every ounce of his self-control

to keep from breaking Ernst's pudgy neck. "You killed Bart and kidnapped Erica expecting to learn something she didn't even know?"

He shrugged. "Bart wasn't supposed to die. Too bad. By the time we gave your bride sodium Pentothal and found out that she never knew what Bart had found, it was too late. I'd given up hope of ever finding it."

"And then Mr. Kilgore's statue turned up," Erica said, "and it started again."

"You thought you had another chance," Shadow said. "Where'd you get the statue, Kilgore?"

"You should know, Shadow. You're the one who sold it to me."

That came from out of nowhere. "And where'd I get it?"

"From Conner Preston," Ernst replied.

Silence cut through the room like a shaft of ice. Shadow couldn't keep the disbelief from his voice. "You think I bought it from Conner Preston?"

Something wasn't right here. He still couldn't be certain who the players were, but one thing he couldn't chance was the possibility that Erica would be hurt.

"How can you be certain it came from me, Kilgore?"

"You called me," he explained. "You said you had it and you were willing to make a deal. I wanted to meet in person, but you refused. You sent the statue by special messenger. Karl authenticated it on the spot and I paid your man."

Karl kicked Conner's gun away. "Let's quit dancing around the truth, Mr. Conner Preston. The others are fools. I've known all along that Preston and Shadow are one and the same. Bart bragged to me about your special skills, the ones that earned you the name Shadow."

Erica couldn't hold back a cry of dismay. Shadow was about to be unmasked. She couldn't let that happen because he'd come to help her. Frantically she searched for a way to protect the man she loved. "What? You're all crazy. Conner isn't Shadow. And Shadow never found the statue."

The ambassador came to Erica's side. "Then you must tell them, Erica. Who found the Virgin?"

Shadow took a step toward Erica, then stopped as Ernst raised his gun, pointing it directly at Erica's head. "I don't think you want to do that, Preston."

"I can't let you take the blame for something you didn't do," she said desperately.

All the men were staring at Erica in disbelief.

"Then tell them," the ambassador urged.

"All right," she said with a gulp. "I'll tell you the truth. I found the Virgin. I sold it to Mr. Kilgore."

"But it was a man who called me, Erica."

"It was a friend. I paid him to deliver the message and the statue."

"Impossible," Ernst sputtered. "You couldn't have known where it was. We gave you truth serum. You would have given us the location."

Ernst cocked the hammer on his gun. "I don't

believe you. You're protecting somebody, but so long as you have what I want, I don't suppose it matters."

For the second time in his life, Conner felt real fear. For the second time someone he loved was standing up to a man with a gun. What in hell was Erica doing, claiming to have what Ernst wanted? There was no way she could have found the treasure. In trying to protect him, she was putting herself in danger.

It was the scene at the little church all over again. If he didn't stop her, they'd both end up dead. But any sudden move could result in the same thing. Better to keep the man talking.

"Don't try it, Ernst," Shadow said calmly. "Erica is making all this up to save Preston."

Ernst growled and moved back to Shadow. He jabbed his pistol hard against his back. "I've heard enough nonsense. I'm losing my patience."

Erica tapped the legs of her chair up and down, struggling to free herself, drawing the light and the attention of all the onlookers. "You don't understand, Professor. I know where the book is—or where it's supposed to be."

"Don't do this, Erica," Shadow snapped. "Ernst is too smart to buy your story."

"Why would I lie? All he wants is the treasure."

Ernst waited a second before answering. "Why would you lie? I can think of about eight million dollars or so. But you're going to tell me now, aren't you? Otherwise I'm going to start shooting people, beginning with Shadow."

"Erica, that's enough!" Shadow growled. "Nobody believes any of this. It's too late for any more lies. You're wrong, Kilgore. I never sold you the Virgin. As for you, Ernst, if Shadow didn't find the treasure, neither did Preston. Here, Ambassador, you hold the light."

Caught by surprise, Ernst allowed the official to take the light and shine it on the masked intruder.

With every eye riveted on him, Conner peeled the mask away. "You see, Ernst was right about one thing. Shadow and Conner Preston are one and the same. Somebody is counting on you to do the dirty work and you're going to take the blame."

"Don't believe him," Erica cried out. "He's only trying to protect me."

Kilgore turned to Ernst. "I told you kidnapping her wouldn't work. I'm not going to jail for you or anybody else. Just give me my money back and you can have the statue. I don't want any part of any of this now."

"Shut up, you fool!" Ernst snapped. His temper was beginning to fray. At that moment the lights came on, blinding them all. Conner saw his chance and jabbed his elbow into Ernst's arm.

The gun went off and Conner felt a slice of fire as a bullet ricocheted off the stone wall and creased his skull. For a minute he saw stars.

"No!" Erica screamed. "I'll get the book. Just don't hurt Conner."

Ernst gestured with his gun. "I thought you would. Untie her, Kilgore."

Once Erica was cut loose, she ran to Conner. "Is it bad?" she asked.

"No. It's just a flesh wound. Now, let me handle this before somebody is really hurt."

Erica gave him a disbelieving smile. "Somebody already is. Get me a phone, Mr. Kilgore."

"Why do you need a phone?" Kilgore asked, sending a nervous look at Karl Ernst.

"Shadow has to call his assistant and make sure the book is where it's supposed to be."

"Erica—" Conner began, "I'm not—"

Ernst swung at the back of Conner's head with the butt of his pistol and Conner collapsed.

Erica stood. "Give me the phone."

From somewhere in the shadows Kilgore produced a cell phone and handed it to Erica. She punched in Mac's number, saying a silent prayer that he would understand what she was telling him and go along with her ploy.

"Sterling," Erica said, calmly speaking over Mac's voice, "this is Erica. I'm calling for Shadow. He wants you to know that the wedding will take place at my home tomorrow, as we planned. Did you send the book to Tennessee?"

Erica nodded at Karl Ernst.

"Good. Charter a private plane for us. We'll need to seat six passengers: the committee, Conner Preston, a doctor, and me. Conner's been—"

"Enough!" Ernst roared, jerking the phone

from Erica's hand. "Sterling, you'd better not try anything funny. I've shot two men and I still have a full clip of bullets I won't mind using."

Karl listened for a moment, smiled, then with a flick of his thumb broke the connection and handed the phone back to Kilgore. "Let's go. He says he'll take care of everything. Apparently we're going to a Christmas wedding. We're already ten years late."

ELEVEN

On the way to the airport, Erica sat between Conner and Karl Ernst. Though he sat totally erect, dried blood etched Conner's hairline, reminding Erica that he'd been shot. She had the feeling that he was remaining upright through sheer willpower. She remembered a time when only willpower kept her going.

Ten years ago she'd lost the man she loved and the child they'd created. The pain had been overwhelming and it had never completely disappeared. She hadn't allowed herself to hope that Mac would send Conner to help her. But he had, and once she'd seen him he'd slid right back into her life and rekindled both the love and the anguish.

Since then she'd been on an emotional roller coaster. She'd covered her pain with anger over his abandonment. Then without her being able to stop it, the anger had changed, dissolving into a stronger emotion. She couldn't say *they'd* fallen in love again because she couldn't be certain how Conner felt. But for her the love was still there where it always had been.

The only anger that remained came from a deep regret for all the time they'd lost. She couldn't help but fear that new loss loomed over them once more. Something bad would happen unless she came up with a way to stop it. People were being shot again. First Bart, then the ambassador, now Conner.

Erica had hoped by promising Professor Ernst the return of the book, Mac could find a way to rescue them. But her wonderful, foolish Conner had tried to protect her by giving up the most important thing in his life—his identity. What would happen when they arrived on Lookout Mountain and there was no book?

The limo entered the airport's General Aviation area, where all charter flights originated. Because it was Christmas Eve, the private center was practically deserted. There were no happy people awaiting the arrival of loved ones, no passengers dashing to board planes, their arms filled with Christmas packages. Instead, the offices were dark and the counters vacant.

Longingly Erica remembered her lovely Christmas tree and the night she and Conner had spent in each other's arms. They'd shared that wonderful moment, but now it was gone. Unless a miracle happened, she was about to lose Conner a second time and she didn't know if she could bear it.

Brighton Kilgore, who'd apparently received final instructions by phone somewhere en route, directed them to the waiting area, then moved into the office, where he was conferring with the pilot. Erica hadn't missed the light nod the pilot had given Conner when they arrived. She let out a sigh of relief. Mac had sent him.

She glanced around the area, wishing they weren't so isolated. Any thought of escape was negated by the increasingly nervous Karl Ernst. Karl kept his gun inside his coat, but there was never any question that it was there and ready for use.

Finally, the pilot led them to his plane and opened the door, letting down the steps. Inside, a second man waited. "Sterling sent me," he said to Conner as they boarded, then turned toward Karl. "I'm the doctor. Who's the wounded man?"

"No doctor!" Ernst pulled his gun from beneath his topcoat.

But the doctor ignored him, turning his piercing black eyes on Conner, whose wound was more obvious now in the light. "I'll just have a look while the pilot is getting takeoff instructions. Please sit down, sir."

Conner dropped into the seat nearest the door, hoping that Erica would remain nearby. Maybe, with a diversion . . . But Karl squelched that idea by shoving Erica farther into the plane.

"All right," Ernst snapped. "Hurry up."

The doctor opened his bag and pulled out a

packet of alcohol-soaked pads. "Quite a hen egg you have there."

"Yeah, the hen used the butt of a gun," Conner joked.

The doctor ripped open a pad. "This is going to sting." He moved around so that his back was to Ernst as he proceeded to clean Conner's wound. As he worked, he let his jacket fall open, revealing a gun in a holster beneath his shoulder. "You're a lucky man. An inch to the left and you might not be here."

Conner's confidence took a boost. With the pilot and the doctor, it stood three to three.

"I'll give you an antibiotic injection and treat your wound. That'll hold you until we reach Chattanooga, but I'd like to get you to a hospital once we're there. You may have suffered a concussion."

"No hospital!" Karl's voice bordered on hysteria. "You'll do whatever he needs. Let's go." He withdrew his gun and brandished it at the pilot.

With no evidence of fear, the pilot moved forward and buckled himself into the captain's chair.

"Now," Ernst directed, "you two, Preston and Ms. Fallon. Sit up front, where I can see you."

Conner rose, a bit unsteady, and followed Erica. They slid into two seats backed against the cockpit. The doctor took one of the chairs opposite them and the ambassador the other. Kilgore sat in the rear, leaving Karl to roam about.

"Don't do anything funny," Karl advised the pilot. "Just fly us to Chattanooga."

After an exchange with the tower, the plane moved toward the runway, where it was forced to sit for nearly half an hour before getting clearance to take off.

"What's holding us up?" Karl demanded, becoming more agitated with every second of the delay.

"Sorry. The charter services aren't busy, but this is one of the heaviest travel days of the year for the commercial airlines. We just have to wait our turn. I know your situation and I'm doing the best I can."

Conner leaned his head against the seat and closed his eyes, trying to shut out the pain. How had he let this happen? And he was responsible. He'd been sent to protect Erica, but he'd allowed his love for her to interfere with his mission.

Now Shadow's identity had been revealed as a result of his failure. No matter. He'd stand in the middle of Times Square and shout his secret to the world to protect Erica. But he was no nearer solving the mysterious appearance of the statue than he had been to begin with. The only thing he was certain of was that Erica hadn't been involved. Not this time. Not ten years ago.

He squeezed her hand.

Even the headache that was pounding against the back of his skull wasn't punishment enough for his lapse in judgment. Shadow would have considered the risks and countered them before they happened. Of all the close calls he'd experienced since Bart's death, this was the first time it was personal.

Though he admired Erica's quick thinking in calling Mac and pretending she was talking to Sterling, he felt damned helpless not being able to do it himself. He glanced at the ambassador, who seemed to be handling their plight better than might be expected. Kilgore looked worried. Perhaps he was reconsidering his loyalties.

Conner held Erica's hand and considered all that had happened. He kept going back to Erica's doodles, to the heart around their names. "I saw your note by the phone," he whispered under his breath.

"You did?"

"No talking to each other," Karl said.

"What about talking to you, Karl?" Conner asked.

Karl moved from the rear of the plane to the remaining vacant seat across the table from Conner and Erica. "Only if you have something to say that I want to hear."

Were he alone, Conner would have rushed Karl. He'd faced greater odds without a thought. But they were in an airplane and Erica was there. And that changed everything.

There was another factor that held Conner back. There was the possibility that he might at last learn the truth about his brother's death. For now he'd bide his time. Sometimes a man about to crack under pressure could be lulled into revealing more than he intended. "Did you ever see Bart's book, Karl?"

"No. He never showed it to me. I was his adviser and he kept it from me. But I know he had it. Bart always wore a backpack. That night before he was killed it was stuffed full, but he wouldn't take it off."

Conner pinched the bridge of his nose and rubbed his eyes. "That was when you knew he'd found the treasure?"

Karl smiled. "Yes, he told me he thought he was close to finding it. I tried to get him to take me there, but he was very nervous, worried about his responsibility and the law. He left my office for the embassy. He didn't want to do anything to spoil his brother's wedding. He promised that he'd show me what he'd found—after the wedding."

Conner held on to his anger with every ounce of his control. "But you couldn't wait. You killed him."

"No!" Karl snapped, almost as if he were trying to convince himself. "I had nothing to do with his death. The assassins were militants, political misfits. I wouldn't have hurt Bart. I'd be killing the goose before he laid the golden egg. He would have made me famous. Bart wouldn't have wanted his discovery to be lost. I knew that. He promised."

Conner turned his gaze on Erica's employer. "Did you see the book, Ambassador?"

"No, I didn't," he answered.

"And Erica never saw it," Conner went on.

"Wouldn't it be ironic if he hadn't made a record at all? If all this were some kind of hoax?"

Ernst's face drew into a grim smile. "No. I thought that for a long time. When I saw the statue I knew that it was part of the missing artwork."

Kilgore, who'd remained quiet up to now, finally joined in the conversation. "So who did find the treasure?"

Karl Ernst waved his gun at Conner and leaned forward. "Yes. Who? Was it our lovely Erica who claims to have used it to bring Conner back into her life? Or was it Mr. Preston? You know what I think? I think it doesn't matter. I will have my answer soon, won't I?"

Erica shook her head sadly. "You're sick, Mr. Ernst. There's no way you can get away with this. There are too many of us who know the truth."

"But that's the beauty of it all," Karl said. "Bart's death was ten years ago and it's already been covered up by the military. Now we have an ambassador, an international businessman, a millionaire, and a German official involved in a plot to steal treasures? Nobody's going to believe that. We won't be greedy. Nobody knows exactly how much there is. We'll turn over enough of the artifacts to make the international art community happy."

"Yes," Kilgore said eagerly. "In the end, we'll all get what we want."

"Except Bart," Conner said. "You know I'm not going to let you sweep this under the rug."

"Then you can think about this," Karl snapped.

"I have Erica and I have you. One of you will produce the book or"—his voice grew deadly quiet—"one of you will die."

Erica shivered. Conner felt it and knew that Ernst had been pushed as far as it was safe to push him. For now Conner needed to think, plan, and hope that Mac had time to work out something on the mountain.

"You're holding all the cards now, Ernst. But we're not there yet. How long is the flight?" Conner asked the pilot, reaching out to take Erica's hand.

"About another hour and a half."

Conner yawned. "Well, I don't know about the rest of you, but I'm feeling a little rocky. If I'm going treasure hunting, I could use some sleep."

"Good idea," Erica said. "I'll turn out the light."

Conner adjusted their seat so that it tilted back and drew Erica against him, shutting his eyes.

Beside him, Erica laid her cheek against his shoulder and followed suit. She wished they could talk. She wished she knew what he was planning. She wished they were back in New Orleans eating chocolate muffins. She wished it was ten years ago and they were planning their wedding.

But it was now and, in spite of the precarious position in which they'd found themselves, Erica felt warm and safe, as if she'd finally come home. Her last waking thought was of Conner. She wondered where he had been that morning when the ambassador called.

Erica roused when the plane touched down in Chattanooga. With Conner wounded and weak, she couldn't believe that she'd actually slept.

"Is it true?" he whispered in her ear.

She turned a questioning look toward him.

"On your notepad. Is it still Erica and Conner?"

"Be quiet!" Karl Ernst backed away from the pilot and turned his gun on Conner. "No whispering."

"Sorry," Conner said in a tight voice. "I was just reassuring Erica."

"But I'm the one who should be reassuring you," Erica said, ignoring Ernst. "The answer is yes. Maybe it's just the Christmas spirit."

She couldn't say it any plainer than that without baring her heart to the world.

"I love the Christmas spirit," he said with an attempt at a wicked smile. "Erica, Christmas, and chocolate, what a combination."

Runway instructions crackled over the radio. The pilot complied. The plane slowed its speed and coasted to a stop.

"Check out the windows, Kilgore," Ernst said, backing toward the door.

Kilgore complied. "Don't see anybody or anything. The place looks deserted."

"Good, open the door."

"Wait," the pilot instructed. "This isn't our dock. We're on the other side."

"Here!" Ernst insisted. "We're getting out here."

The pilot turned off the engine and Kilgore opened the door, letting the steps down.

Karl stood beside the portal, just out of view, his finger on the trigger. "You first, Kilgore."

Nervously, Kilgore peered out, then moved down the steps. "All clear!" he called out.

Moments later they were walking across the dark runway toward the terminal, passing several offices before they found the door to the central area. But all Karl's precautions seemed unnecessary. They seemed to be the only ones around. Outside the front door a van waited. The key was in the switch.

"You drive, Kilgore," Ernst directed.

"Now, just a minute, Ernst. I'm getting a little tired of you running the show. You drive."

Conner didn't like the way things were going. Ernst had grabbed Erica once again. They'd left the pilot behind and there was no sign of Mac. Conner was weaker than he thought and he didn't have to be told his reflexes were off. Fortunately, nobody had frisked him so they were unaware of the second gun he'd jabbed into his boot. Still, even with the doctor's help, he could see no way of using it without endangering Erica.

"Get in!" Ernst screamed.

"I'll drive," Conner volunteered. "If Erica will direct me."

"Do it." Ernst waved his gun toward the van. "You two sit in the front. I'll sit behind Erica. If anything, anything goes wrong, she's dead."

Conner crawled into the van. With an ironic grin he fastened his seat belt and watched as Erica did the same. What did it matter if they were buckled in? A bullet would be just as fatal as a car crash.

As they drove through the city, Conner focused his attention on the mountain. There'd be no ride up the Incline Railroad this trip. On Christmas Eve they probably shut the sightseeing down early anyway.

Erica directed him along the river to the long, curving road leading up. Already darkness covered the mountain like a gauzy cape. The lights of the Christmas decorations peeked through the low-hanging clouds like pieces of costume jewelry.

Conner drove slowly because he was beginning to think that he had a concussion. His vision blurred occasionally, forcing him to blink repeatedly to clear away the fuzzy spots. The tension inside the van increased steadily as they snaked upward.

"Faster," Karl said.

"This isn't easy," Conner argued gently. "The road is narrow and the fog is rolling in. I don't think you want me to drive off the side of the mountain, do you?"

At that moment they came to an open space,

where the trees, bare of leaves, looked as if they'd been poked into the side of the hill like picks in a dead floral arrangement. The entire valley was visible below. There were no guard rails and no wide shoulders to protect a vehicle.

Karl cleared his throat.

"Drive carefully, Conner," the ambassador said. "Be quiet, Karl. You're too close now to blow it with impatience."

Karl gave the ambassador a quick look and let out a long breath. "Just get us there."

Finally, they reached the top and, with Erica's instructions, the street on which she lived. Navigating was made more difficult by cars parked along its side. This was Christmas Eve, the time for family dinners and out of town company. They'd have to be careful not to catch an innocent bystander in the showdown.

And that was what Conner was preparing for—a showdown. He wasn't sure about the ambassador, but he and the doctor had to overpower two men who expected to find the location of a treasure worth millions of dollars.

He pulled the van into the narrow space in front of the garage and killed the engine. "Well, there are no lights inside, Erica. I guess we can assume that we're celebrating Christmas alone."

"Give Kilgore the key," Ernst instructed. "We'll wait here until you check it out."

"Wait a minute," Kilgore argued. "I told you I

wanted out. I'm not going in there by myself. Suppose—"

Ernst waved the gun. "I said, check it out."

"I'll go with you," the ambassador said, sliding the van door open and climbing down slowly.

Kilgore followed. "Great. A lot of help you'll be if someone is waiting for us."

Erica gave out a little sound of impatience. "There is no one in the house. Who would be there?"

Moments later the door opened and light poured through every window.

Conner hadn't known what to expect, but he was disappointed when Kilgore called out, "Everything's clear."

Ernst stepped out and once again grabbed Erica by the arm. "You walk with me, Erica. Just so Mr. Preston doesn't get any fancy ideas. We don't want anybody else shot, do we?"

So much for Conner's plan to shove Erica inside and take Karl outside the door. He and the doctor stepped into the foyer and moved toward the study at the back of the house. Kilgore was studying the fireplace. "Damn, it's cold in here. Where's the thermostat?"

"Doesn't matter," Ernst snapped. "We aren't going to be here long enough for that. Get in the middle of the room—all of you." He continued to hold Erica as the others complied. "Now, you get the book, Erica."

She'd run out of time. Mac hadn't been able to

help. There was nothing to do but admit the truth. "I don't have it."

Ernst lifted the gun. "No more stalling, Ms. Fallon." He took off the safety and pointed it at Conner.

"That's enough, Karl." The ambassador stepped between Ernst and the others. "So far nobody has been killed. You can't let this go any further."

Ernst shook off the ambassador's words. "What do you mean, I can't go any further? I'm not taking any more orders from you. None of this has worked out like you planned. And I'm not taking the blame for shooting anybody."

Erica gasped. "You, Mr. Ambassador? I don't believe that. You were shot!"

The diplomat let out a shallow breath and nodded. "I'm afraid so, Erica. A necessary action, meant to make you understand the seriousness of our request. It was either you or me. I'm very sorry it had to come to this, Erica, but I'd like the book now."

Conner wished he could save Erica from what was coming. But it had to play itself out. "How'd they get to you, Ambassador? From what I've learned, you're a man easily led, but a servant of the people involved in international theft? Is that a new part of your diplomatic job description?"

"Job description?" The old man spat out bitterly. "Where in the job description does it tell you what you're supposed to do when your life's work is suddenly taken away, and you're offered retirement or reassignment to a nothing little country that nobody has ever heard of?"

"I always believed you cared about me," Erica said softly.

"I did. I still do. In spite of Karl's contention otherwise, I was satisfied that you didn't know about Bart's discovery."

Conner didn't like the sound of the diplomat's voice. It was thready and weak. Even in the watery light, Conner could see that his color was ashen. Ambassador Collins had become a desperate old man who was past being a threat. Still, Conner couldn't let up now.

"So when did this unholy alliance with Kilgore and Ernst begin?" Conner asked.

"What difference does it make now?" He propped himself on the table at the end of the couch. "Karl has been searching for the hiding place ever since Bart turned over the piece of broken marble. He identified it immediately as being from a statue stolen from a church in Italy. But Bart swore there was nothing else in that passage."

Erica gave a troubled laugh. "He was right. Conner and I were there when he found the marble. That was all we found."

She noticed the doctor moving back into the shadows and slowly toward the table where Kilgore stood. She needed to keep the two men talking. "You knew about Bart's black book from the beginning, didn't you, Ambassador Collins? And it was your idea for those men to pretend to be Green Berets and kidnap me."

"Yes. I knew about the book," the ambassador admitted. "I'm very sorry, Erica. I never intended for anyone to be hurt. Then those fools Karl hired got trigger-happy and Bart was killed."

"Hah, let anybody prove it," Karl said.

The ambassador took a weary breath and continued. "Conner was gone and though we searched everywhere, the book had disappeared."

"And that's the real reason you hired me to work for you," Erica said. "You were still looking for Bart's notes."

"In the beginning, yes."

Conner couldn't take a chance on moving. The doctor was almost even with the ambassador. Just a few more seconds. "What about Kilgore's part in all this?" Conner asked.

Karl snorted. "Kilgore's a fool. The statue had to go to somebody who had the money to buy it. We knew he wouldn't ask questions when we told him that it came from Shadow. And we also knew he wouldn't be able to resist showing it off. We counted on somebody coming forward with the truth."

"A fool?" Kilgore rushed toward Karl. "What do you mean, a fool?"

This time there was no storm, no lights, only whatever expertise Conner had spent years developing. Before anybody knew that he'd moved, he caught Ernst's hand, closing around the gun and shoving it toward the ceiling. But the man was stronger than he looked. He let Erica go and turned toward Conner, elbowing him in the chest. As they struggled, both men went down. The gun fired and fell to the floor.

Erica screamed.

"Run, Erica!" Conner yelled as he fell on top of Ernst. "Call 911."

"I've got this one," the doctor called out as he twisted Kilgore's arm behind him.

But Ernst wasn't ready to give up. He kneed Conner in the groin and managed to crawl away. Just as he reached for the gun, Conner put him out with a karate chop to the neck. In a matter of seconds it was all over.

Erica knelt by the ambassador, who lay on the floor, moaning.

"I'm so sorry, Erica," the old man said. "I never meant this to happen. I just wanted to go back to Berlin. If I found the artifacts, they'd have to reward me."

"About Bart's notes, Ambassador," she asked. "Are you convinced that there really was a book with the location of the treasure?"

"Yes, Erica. There really was. I saw it." He gasped and closed his eyes. The front of his shirt was seeping blood.

Erica raised her eyes to meet Conner's. "I think you'd better come over here, Doctor. Karl's shot hit the ambassador. That is, if you're really a doctor."

"I'm really a doctor," he said, turning to the man lying prostrate on the Oriental rug.

Erica, still shaking at the possibility of what could have happened, folded her arms across her chest and held on to her elbows.

"So where did Kilgore get the statue?" she asked.

"From me," the ambassador replied in a thready voice. "The night that Bart came to see me, he brought not only his book, but two statues that proved his claim. He left this one with me for safe-keeping. Then he was killed, and the secret hiding place died with him."

Erica looked at the ambassador with sadness in her eyes. "It was you all the time. You knew Mr Kilgore had tried to hire Shadow to look for the treasure. You just didn't know that Shadow had turned him down. So you had the statue sent to Brighton in Shadow's name. Then Professor Ernst authenticated its history—all so that Brighton would fund your committee. The committee would make the search legitimate enough to smoke out the diary, either from me or Preston."

Conner shook his head. "So many things could have gone wrong. How could you believe your plan would work?"

Ernst groaned and struggled to sit up, leaning his back against the wall. "It did work. That book is out there somewhere. I would have found it if it weren't for you, Preston."

At that moment, flashing blue lights and sirens

sounded outside the door, announcing the arrival of the police and an ambulance.

The police explained that the house had been wired. They'd been listening to everything that had happened. Conner turned over Ernst's gun while Ernst and Kilgore were placed under arrest. The paramedics loaded the ambassador into the ambulance. At the last moment, one of the officers shoved Conner into the departing vehicle.

"No!" Erica shouted. "I'm coming with you."

As the door was closing, Conner called out to Erica, "Wait here for me. I'll be back."

The caravan of blinking lights snaked back down the road, leaving Erica alone on top of the mountain. She looked out at the moon peeking through the clouds and felt a drop of moisture roll down her face.

It was Christmas Eve and she was alone.

TWELVE

Erica glanced at the clock over the mantel for the hundredth time. It was almost three o'clock in the morning. Mac had called to say that the report from the hospital was good, but Conner had been gone for over three hours.

"Idiot. You know that hospitals insist on keeping a patient with a concussion overnight."

But he could have called.

He wasn't going to call. He'd protected her as Mac had asked him to do and he'd found out what happened to Bart. She'd never see him again. Why should she expect to?

But, dammit, he cared about her. Oh, he hadn't said the words, but she knew. They were good together. Each of them made the other stronger. She was no longer an unwanted child, no longer an adult who made things run smoothly for someone else. She was Erica Fallon, Dragon Lady. Shadow's Dragon Lady.

Erica let out a deep sigh. The past two days had shown her that action solved problems and the time had come for her to take some in her own life. Maybe she'd start by going to the hospital first thing in the morning. This time she wouldn't give up. If Conner wouldn't come to her, she'd go to him.

Erica stood and began turning off all the lights. Though the house was finally warm, she shivered. She crossed her arms over her chest, rubbing them slowly. She wondered if she'd ever feel warm again.

She moved down the hall to the front door and turned off the porch light. Then she started back toward the kitchen, pausing for a moment when she reached the spot where she'd been sitting the night Conner came.

As if on command, a shaft of moonlight cut through the clouds and focused on the deck, catching a man in its beam. He was dressed all in black, from his head to his feet. Except for a red cap with a band of white fur around it.

Erica's heart stopped.

The door opened.

"I don't know who you are," she whispered, "but if you're not Shadow, you'd better be Santa."

He closed the door and came slowly down the hall, a bell jingling like spurs with every step. "Have you been a good little girl?"

"Would that get me what I want?"

"Depends on what you want," he said.

"I don't think you can fit it in your bag."

"Try me."

They were standing only inches apart when she answered. "I want to get married."

"So do I. To anyone in particular?"

"Oh, yes. I've had my eye on the groom for ten years. If he'll still have me."

"He'd be very honored to have you. Will tomorrow be soon enough?"

"I guess it will have to be as long as we don't have to wait until after the ceremony to start our honeymoon."

He pulled off his Santa cap and dropped it on the floor. He hooked his finger beneath her chin and tilted her head up. The moment shimmered between them, the tension dissolving her very bones.

"God, I still want you," he said.

"Lust, I believe you called it. Is that enough?"

"Hell no, lust isn't enough. I want a woman who'll nurse my wounds when I'm hurt, who'll take on the world if she thinks she can save my life, who waits for me even when I've let her down in the past. What do you want?"

She could have given him a laundry list of the things she loved about him: his compassion, his dedication, his willingness to risk his life for her. Instead, she simply said, "You."

Erica could feel his need, the intensity of his holding back. The air around them seemed to get hotter. She gasped and swayed toward him, no longer able to tolerate the distance between them.

Then Conner kissed her, long and deep.

"There's never been another woman for me, Dragon Lady," he whispered. "We've wasted too much time. I want to be beside you, inside you, with you for the rest of my life."

But he didn't touch her, except to support her waist with his big hands. He seemed intent on drawing out every nuance of heat that was scorching her very skin. It was as if he knew she was about to explode.

He pulled back and looked down at her, his blue eyes stormy in the half-light, his lips grim.

"What's wrong, Conner?"

"Not a thing. For the first time in a very long time, everything is right." He lifted his knee and shucked one boot, then the other, and finally, his socks, his gaze planted firmly on Erica all the while.

She glanced down at the floor and Conner's bare feet, then smiled. "No fair, you're getting a head start."

His lips relaxed, curling into a smile that made the blood in her veins churn. "We can't have that, can we?" His gaze drifted to her breasts and down. "No zipper?"

She shook her head.

He caught the bottom of her sweater and pulled it up, bending her back across his arm as his lips feasted on breasts that were covered by a scrap of lace.

Before Conner had been the leader. This time Erica pushed him away and moments later, in the faint light of the one lamp still glowing in the kitchen, she stood before him totally nude.

He whispered her name and reached for her.

"No, Conner. Let me. We don't have our tree and there is no snow, but it's Christmas. You're exactly what I wanted Santa to bring me. Let me unwrap my present."

She removed his sweater, unfastened his pants, and slid the zipper down. As he drew in a deep breath, she took him by the hand and led him up the stairs, kissing him upward, one step at a time.

But every time he tried to pull her closer, she stopped him. "Not yet. Anticipation is half the fun."

At the top of the stairs she hooked her thumbs inside his jeans and briefs, sliding them down, freeing his erection to be tortured by her lips and her tongue.

Conner groaned, and pulled her up. "I've had just about as much anticipation as I can handle for one night, darling."

She laughed and danced away from him and down the corridor into the bedroom, where she'd once come to hide from the world. Conner followed, closing the door behind him, throwing the room into total darkness.

At that moment the clouds outside parted, allowing the light of a silver moon to flood through the crocheted valance at her window. Suddenly the room was cast with a delicate pattern that looked like snow. The wind whistled against the house, moving the curtain slightly, turning the design into a swirling storm of white.

"Oh, Conner. Thank you."

Too filled with emotion to reply, Conner lifted her in his arms and laid her on the bed. And there, amid nature's canopy of light, Conner Preston made love to the woman who would at last become his wife.

There were no words to describe their coming together, except her cry of ecstasy at his touch. She threaded her fingers into his hair and pulled him against her.

As Conner thrust himself inside her, Erica lifted her hips to meet him. Conner gritted his teeth and held on with every ounce of control he possessed. But it had been too long and his need too great. He couldn't hold back his intense release, and it took him a moment to realize that she was climaxing with him.

As he came back down, he felt her tight around him, still holding on and he opened his eyes in wonder. "Wow, lady! If this is what happens when you live in the clouds, I may never want to leave."

"That's good," she said in a light, breathless voice, "because I don't intend to let you."

"But it happened so fast I didn't—I mean, you . . ."

"Oh, yes I did." She flexed her muscles, setting off a throb of desire through their still-connected bodies. Catching his face in her hands, she drew him down for a long, deep kiss. "And I think I could do it again."

She did.

And so did he.

At last the moon moved behind the trees and their fairy tale setting faded to black. Conner slid off her, gathering her against him.

"I feel as if I'm floating," he said with surprise in his voice.

Floating? "Conner." She rose on one elbow, looking down at him. "I didn't ask, are you all right? I mean your concussion. This could have killed you."

"I would have died happy. Before that happens, Erica, I want to say that I love you. I always did. I still do."

"And I love you, Conner Preston. I always have. Now, tell me the truth. Did they really think you were well enough to be released from the hospital?"

"Conner Preston was told to stay. But Shadow always gets in and out of anyplace he wants to."

"Shouldn't you be resting?"

"I told you once I believed in the kiss-it-and-make-it-better method of treatment. I can assure you, I'm one hundred percent cured. Well, maybe only ninety-nine. We'd better keep working on it."

"Tell me what happened." She snuggled back into the curve of his shoulder.

"They took Ernst and Kilgore into custody. I

think Kilgore will be out before morning, but his collecting days may be numbered."

"What about the ambassador?"

"They don't know yet. This time the wound was in his chest. He's an old man. My guess is that he doesn't want to survive."

Erica felt bad about what had happened, but when she considered the full picture, she couldn't forgive the ambassador for what he'd done. Though not directly responsible for Bart's death, the ambassador had to share the blame.

"Do you think it was Ambassador Collins who arranged to intercept my letter to you, Conner?"

"Collins or the base commander. I guess we won't ever know."

"But Ambassador Collins wasn't all bad, Conner," she persisted. "He really did help me. Why?"

"Who knows? Maybe it was out of genuine concern and maybe it was as a kind of insurance policy for himself. I think he must have had hope that someday you'd produce Bart's book. Why'd you stay with him?"

"I told you. He really needed me. I liked my job and the embassy was like a family. They made me feel secure."

Conner turned slightly, bringing his free arm down and capturing one breast with his fingertips. "But you have a new life now, with me."

Erica had never wanted anything more. But there was still one truth left unsaid. She couldn't let Conner marry her without knowing it all.

"There's something I have to tell you, Conner. You never got my letter so you never knew . . . I was pregnant."

"Pregnant?" His fingertips stilled. "You were carrying my child?"

"Yes. I didn't know where you were. I wrote to tell you about the baby and that I was going to Paris. I got an apartment and I waited. And I waited. But you never came."

"Son of a—I swear, Erica. I never knew."

"I know that now."

"The ambassador said something about a hospital, about you being ill. Was that it? What happened?"

"At six months I developed some kind of infection. The doctors did everything they could, but I lost the baby."

"I should have been there. I would have come."

She sighed. "I was very sick for a long time. Then the ambassador found me and took me into the embassy. His wife was still living then. They gave me a home and the pain gradually eased."

He caught her fingertips, pressing them against his lips. "I'm so sorry, Erica. It must have been terrible. I don't know why you'd let me within ten feet of you after what I did."

"But I didn't blame you. I knew you held me responsible for Bart's death. You believed that I'd changed my mind about the wedding. I—I thought I was protecting you. If I hadn't gone with those men, Bart wouldn't have died. You can't imagine how guilty I felt."

"And I didn't come back to you because of my own guilt. I couldn't even go to Bart's funeral. For months I didn't want to live myself. The only way I could face my failure was to blame you. I was alive, but Bart was dead.

"It was all I could think about. That and you. I should have known something was wrong, but I couldn't allow myself to have you." He buried his face in her hair. "Losing you was my punishment."

"You lost Bart and me. I lost you and our child. Don't you think we've lost enough? Bart would want you to get past this tragedy and go on living. The thing I regret most is that Bart will never get the credit for what he found."

A moment passed in silence.

"There are still two things I'm wondering about," Conner finally said. "According to the ambassador, Bart brought one of the statues to prove his claim. Where was the other statue?"

"I guess he must have left it behind. Maybe someday someone will find the secret room and all the treasures can be returned to their rightful owners. What's the other question?"

"Paradox, Inc. is still in business, but it looks like Shadow won't be taking on any more secret missions and you don't have a job. Do you have any thoughts on our future?"

"As a matter of fact, I was thinking about completing my degree and maybe . . . maybe finishing

Bart's work. As for Shadow, I see no reason for him to vanish."

"I do. Shadow takes too many risks. I have a wife now and . . . I know it's too soon to talk about it," he said, rimming her nipples with his fingertips, "but there's another thing I'd like us to accomplish."

"What?"

"Another baby. Babies. I want lots of babies. What do you think?"

"I like your plans, Conner. I like you. I think I always knew that we were meant to be together."

"That's why I'm here," he agreed.

"I wish we had our Christmas tree," she said, savoring the idea of her future with Conner.

"It'll still be in our suite when we get back tomorrow."

"We're going back to New Orleans?"

"Of course. We have to open the presents under it."

"I already have the only present I want. But I don't have anything for you."

"Oh, yes, you do," he said, and moved over her. "And I'm going to enjoy it at least once more before morning. By the way, do you have any chocolate in the house?"

The doorbell had been ringing for some time before Erica finally heard it. Groggily, she sat up and reached for her robe.

Conner was beginning to stir as she left the room and started toward the front door.

"Yes?"

A uniformed postal employee was standing outside, holding a large box. "Mrs. Preston?" he asked.

Erica frowned, then nodded.

"Special delivery package for you. It's pretty heavy. Better let me set it inside."

She stepped back as he put it in the foyer.

"Thank you," she managed to say.

"Sure thing. Merry Christmas."

"Merry Christmas to you," she answered as she shut the door behind him.

"Who is it?" Conner's voice came from behind her.

She turned around to see him stumbling into the hallway, zipping his jeans.

"The postman. What kind of silly thing have you done?"

"Not me, not this time. What is it?"

"I don't guess we'll know until we open it. Let's take it to the kitchen."

The package was wrapped in brown paper and postmarked Berlin. The original label had been addressed to Lieutenant and Mrs. Conner Preston, in care of Ambassador Collins, U.S. Embassy, Washington, D.C. That address had been marked through and it had been forwarded to Erica in Tennessee.

Conner lifted an eyebrow, then grabbed a knife

from the drawer and split open the wrapping. Inside was a box covered in yellowed wrapping paper and a card. *To the two people I love most in the world. Be happy, Bart.*

"Bart must have had this with him the morning of the wedding," Conner said softly.

"Where has it been all this time?"

Conner looked at the return address. "It came from the minister who was to marry us. Mac spoke with him and said the old man was sending us something."

They looked at each other, throats too tight to speak.

Finally, Conner ripped off the paper and cut the tape securing the box. Swallowing hard, he wiped his hands on the sides of his jeans and opened it. Peeling away the shredded-up newspaper, he lifted the object.

Erica gasped. "The other Virgin Mary."

Conner shoved the box and paper away and switched on the overhead lights. The second statue was as exquisite as the first. A note was taped to the ornate base. Conner opened it, almost afraid to read what was inside.

I think somebody's been following me for the last two days. If anything happens to me, brother, I'm entrusting you with my discovery. Shadow can follow my directions and find the secret room, even if you can't. I love you, guy. Bart.

Conner handed the note to Erica. "Follow his instructions? What instructions?" He lifted the statue, turning it over and over, studying the work of art. Then he saw a tiny nick beneath the Virgin Mary's feet, almost like an arrow.

He inserted the tip of the knife into the mark and pried. The bottom of the base dropped off, revealing a hollow space, a space containing, "the black book," Conner said.

"It existed all the time," Erica murmured.

Their eyes met and Erica felt their thoughts join. Closure, at last. All the loose ends had been tied up. Now Bart's death stood for something. He'd really found the treasures.

"What shall we do with it?" She asked.

"I'm not sure. Maybe your idea to go treasure hunting is a good one—for Bart. We'll ask Mac. He's a very wise man who knows how to right a wrong."

Conner replaced the statue on its base and slid his arm around Erica. The warm feeling inside his heart expanded, filling him with joy and peace.

"For Bart," Erica agreed. She lifted her face to receive Conner's kiss, a kiss that was tender and warm and promised forever. She knew that she was home at last.

"Now," she said, several moments later, "about that craving for chocolate."

EPILOGUE

"Mac, I need some help."

Lincoln MacAllister recognized the voice of Laura O'Leary. He'd heard it enough in the years since he'd arranged for her to attend law school. He turned away from the glass window overlooking the desert beyond the sanctuary called Shangrila and concentrated on the most famous O'Leary in Chicago.

"What's wrong? Has one of your homeless shelters run out of funds again?"

"No, for an attorney I'm turning into a pretty good fund-raiser. This problem is a little different. You know I've been trying to get to the slumlord responsible for Learytown."

"Yes, I've been reading your accounts. I told you I didn't need written reports of your work."

"You paid for my law degree and helped me open my office. I owe you."

"I'd have been willing to spring for better quarters, if you'd let me."

"No, Learytown is where my family started and where I'm needed. But I've run into a stone wall here."

Mac smiled. Problems were nothing new to Laura. Neither were solutions. She must really be up against it to ask for help. "What can I do?"

"I want an invitation to a masquerade ball."

Lincoln MacAllister smothered a laugh as he prepared to listen to Laura's latest attempt to make the world better. "An invitation to a party? Explain."

"Maybe I ought not to. It might involve breaking the law, and I wouldn't want to get you into trouble. Do you know B. J. Cameron?"

"I know of him."

"Well, he's having a very elegant winter ball, complete with costumes and masks. I need to go."

Mac suspected he was going to regret helping, but this was the first time Laura had ever asked anything personal.

"Why? That doesn't sound like you."

"I'm going straight to the top, or, to put it another way, I'm planning to confront the devil directly."

Mac bit back a smile. She might just do it. He scanned his angel directory. Who did he know in Chicago who owed him?

Of course. He knew of B. J. Cameron, but he was better acquainted with his son Ben. If Laura wanted to go to the ball, she'd get her invitation all right.

Straight from the devil himself.

"I think I can arrange it, Laura. Just sit tight."

Moments later he dialed the proper set of numbers and listened to the phone ring.

"Ben, this is Lincoln MacAllister. Wonder if you'd do something for me."

THE EDITORS' CORNER

Begin your holiday celebration early with the four new LOVESWEPT romances coming your way next month. Packed with white-hot emotion, each of these novels is the best getaway from the hustle and bustle typical of this time of year. So set aside a few hours for yourself, cuddle up with the books, and enjoy!

THE DAMARON MARK: THE LION, LOVESWEPT #814, is the next enticing tale in Fayrene Preston's bestselling Damaron Mark series. Lion Damaron is too gorgeous to be real, a walking heartbreaker leaning against a wrecked sports car, when Gabi St. Armand comes to his rescue! She doesn't dare let his seductive smile persuade her he is serious, but flirting with the wealthy hunk is reckless fun—and the only way she can disguise the desire that scorches her very soul. Fayrene Preston beguiles once more with her irresistible tale of unexpected, impossible love that simply must be.

TALL, DARK, AND BAD is the perfect description for the hero in Charlotte Hughes's newest LOVESWEPT, #815. He storms her grandmother's dinner party like a warrior claiming his prize, but when Cooper Garrett presses Summer Pettigrew against the nearest wall and captures her mouth, she has no choice but to surrender. He agrees to play her fiancé in a breathless charade, but no game of let's pretend can be this steamy, this erotic. Get set for a story that's both wickedly funny and wildly arousing, as only Charlotte Hughes can tell it.

For her holiday offering, Peggy Webb helps Santa decide who's **NAUGHTY AND NICE**, #816. Benjamin Sullivan III knows trouble when he spots it in a redhead's passionate glare, but figuring out why Holly Jones is plotting against the town's newest arrival is a mystery too fascinating to ignore! How can she hunger so for a handsome scoundrel? Holly wonders, even as she finds herself charmed, courted, and carried away by Ben's daredevil grin. Award-winning author Peggy Webb makes mischief utterly sexy and wins hearts with teasing tenderness!

Suzanne Brockmann's seductive and inventive romance tangles readers in **THE KISSING GAME**, LOVESWEPT, #817. Allowing Simon Hunt to play her partner on her latest assignment probably isn't Frankie Paresky's best idea ever, but the P.I. finds it just as hard as most women do to tell him no! When a chase to solve a long-ago mystery sparks a sizzling attraction between old friends, Frankie wavers between pleasure and panic. Simon's the best bad boy she's ever known, and he just might turn out to be the man she'll always love. Suzanne Brockmann delivers pure pleasure from the first page to the last.

Happy reading!

With warmest wishes,

Beth de Guzman

Shauna Summers

Beth de Guzman   Shauna Summers

Senior Editor   Editor

P.S. Watch for these Bantam women's fiction titles coming in December: Join *New York Times* bestselling author Sandra Brown for **BREAKFAST IN BED**, available in mass-market. Kay Hooper, nationally bestselling author of *AMANDA*, weaves a tale of mystery when two strangers are drawn together by one fatal moment in **AFTER CAROLINE**. The long-out-of-print classic **LOVE'S A STAGE**, by the beloved writing team Sharon and Tom Curtis, is back for your pleasure. And for her Bantam Books debut, Patricia Coughlin presents **LORD SAVAGE**. Don't miss the previews of these exceptional novels in next month's LOVESWEPTs.

If you're into the world of computers and would like current information on Bantam's women's fiction, visit our Web site, ISN'T IT ROMANTIC, at the following address: **http://www.bdd.com/ romance.**

And immediately following this page, sneak a peek at the Bantam women's fiction titles on sale *now*!

Don't miss these extraordinary titles
by your favorite Bantam authors!

On sale in October:

SHADOWS AND LACE
by Teresa Medeiros

THE MARRIAGE WAGER
by Jane Ashford

She was a slave to his passion . . . but he was
the master of her heart

SHADOWS
AND LACE

a stunning novel of captive love
by national bestseller

Teresa Medeiros

*With one roll of the dice, the shameful deed was done.
Baron Lindsey Fordyce had gambled and lost, and now his
beautiful daughter, Rowena, was about to pay the price.
Spirited away to an imposing castle, the fiery innocent
found herself pressed into the service of a dark and forbidding knight accused of murder . . . and much more.
Handsome, brooding Sir Gareth of Caerleon had spent
years waiting for this chance for revenge. But when he
sought to use the fair Rowena to slay the ghosts of his
tortured past, he never imagined he'd be ensnared in a
silken trap of his own making—slave to a desire he could
never hope to quench. . . .*

Rowena came bursting in like a ray of sunshine cut-
ting through the stale layer of smoke that hung over
the hall. The wild, sweet scent of the moor clung to
her hair, her skin, the handwoven tunic she wore. Her

cheeks were touched with the flushed rose of exertion; her eyes were alight with exuberance.

She ran straight to her father, her words tumbling out faster than the apples dumped from the sack she clutched upside down.

"Oh, Papa, I am ever so happy you've come home! Where did you have the stallion hidden? He is the most beautiful animal I ever saw. Did you truly find your elusive fortune this journey?"

Falling to her knees beside his chair, she pulled a crumpled bunch of heather from her pocket and dumped it in his lap without giving him time to reply.

"I brought your favorite flowers and Little Freddie has promised to cook apples on the coals. They will be hot and sweet and juicy, just as you like them. 'Twill be a hundred times better than any nasty old roasted hare. Oh, Papa, you're home! We thought you were never coming back."

She threw her arms around his waist. The uninhibited gesture knocked the cap from her head to unleash a cascade of wheaten curls.

Fordyce's arms did not move to encircle her. He sat stiff in her embrace. She lifted her face, aware of a silence broken only by the thump of a log shifting on the fire. Her father did not meet her eyes, and for one disturbing moment, she thought she saw his lower lip tremble.

She followed his gaze. Her brothers stood lined up before the hearth in the most ordered manner she had ever seen them. Irwin beamed from the middle of the row.

Bathed in the light of the flickering fire, the stranger stepped out of the shadows. Rowena raised her eyes. From where she knelt, it was as if she was peering up from the bottom of a deep well to meet the eyes of the man who towered over her. His level gaze sent a bolt of raw fear through her, riveting her to the floor as she stared into the face of death itself. A long moment passed before she could pull her eyes away.

"Papa?" she breathed, patting his cool, trembling hand.

He stroked her hair, his eyes distant. "Rowena, I believe 'twould be fitting for you to step outside till we have concluded our dealings."

"You made no mention of a daughter, Fordyce." The stranger's gaze traveled between father and child.

Papa's arm curved around Rowena's shoulders like a shield. The stranger's mocking laughter echoed through the hall. Only Rowena heard Papa's muttered curse as he realized what he had done.

"Your interest is in my sons," Papa hissed, a tiny vein in his temple beginning to throb.

"But *your* interest is not. That much is apparent."

The man advanced and Rowena rose, knowing instinctively that she did not want to be on her knees at this stranger's feet. She stood without flinching to face the wrought links of the silver chain mail that crossed the man's chest. From broad shoulders to booted feet, his garments were as black as the eyes that regarded her with frank scrutiny. She returned his perusal with arms crossed in front of her.

A closer look revealed his eyes were not black, but a deep, velvety brown. Their opacity rendered them inscrutable, but alive with intelligence. Heavy, arched brows added a mocking humor that gave Rowena the impression she was being laughed at, although his expression did not waver. His sable hair was neatly cut, but an errant waviness warned of easy rebellion. His well-formed features were saved from prettiness by an edge of rugged masculinity enhanced by his sheer size. The thought flitted through Rowena's mind that he might be handsome if his face was not set in such ruthless lines.

He reached down and lifted a strand of her hair as if hypnotized at its brightness. The velvety tendril curled around his fingers at the caress.

Rowena's hand slipped underneath her tunic, but before she could bring the knife up to strike, her wrist was twisted in a fearful grip that sent the blade clattering to the stones. She bit her lip to keep from crying out. The man loosed her.

"She has more fire than the rest of you combined." The stranger strode back to the hearth. "I'll take her."

The hall exploded in enraged protest. Papa sank back in the chair, his hand over his eyes.

"You cannot have my sister!" Little Freddie's childish tenor cut through his brothers' cries.

The man leaned against the hearth with a smirk. "Take heart, lad. 'Tis not forever. She is only to serve me for a year."

Rowena looked at Papa. His lips moved with no sound. Her brothers spewed forth dire and violent threats, although they remained in place as if rooted to the stone. She wondered if they had all taken leave of their senses. The stranger's sparkling eyes offered no comfort. They watched her as if delighting in the chaos he had provoked. The tiny lines around them crinkled as he gave her a wink made all the more threatening by its implied intimacy. A primitive thrill of fear shot through her, freezing her questions before they could leave her lips.

Papa's whine carried just far enough to reach the man's ears. "We said sons, did we not?"

The man's booming voice silenced them all. "Nay, Fordyce. We said children. I was to have the use of one of your children for a year."

Rowena's knees went as slack as her jaw. Only the sheer effort of her will kept her standing.

"You cannot take a man's only daughter," said Papa, unable to keep the pleading note from his voice. "Show me some mercy, won't you?"

The knight snorted. "Mercy? What have you ever known of mercy, Fordyce? I've come to teach you of justice."

Papa mustered his courage and banged with force on the arm of the chair. "I will not allow it."

The stranger's hand went to the hilt of the massive sword sheathed at his waist. Beneath the rich linen of his surcoat, the muscles in his arms rippled with the slight gesture. "You choose to fight?" he asked softly.

Lindsey Fordyce hesitated the merest moment. "Rowena, you must accompany this nice man."

Rowena blinked stupidly, thrown off guard by her father's abrupt surrender.

Little Freddie charged forward, an iron pot wielded over his head like a bludgeon. The knight turned with sword drawn. Rowena lunged for his arm, but Papa sailed past both of them and knocked the boy to the ground with a brutal uppercut. Freddie glared at his father, blood trickling from his mouth and nose.

"Don't be an idiot," Papa spat. "He will only kill you, and then he will kill me."

Still wielding his sword, the stranger faced the row of grumbling boys. "If anyone cares to challenge my right to their sister, I shall be more than happy to defend it."

The broad blade gleamed in the firelight. Big Freddie returned the man's stare for a long moment, his callused paws clenched into fists. He turned away and rested his forehead against the warm stones of the hearth.

The stranger's eyes widened as Irwin's plump form stepped forward, trumpet still clutched in hand. Papa took one step toward Irwin, who then plopped his ample bottom on the hearth and studied the trumpet as if seeing it for the first time.

"A wager is a wager." Papa ran his thumbs along the worn gilt of his tattered surcoat. "As you well know, I am a baron and a knight myself—an honorable man."

He sighed as if the burden of his honor was too much for him to bear. The short laugh uttered by the knight was not a pleasant sound.

Papa gently took Rowena's face between his moist palms. "Go with him, Rowena." He swallowed with difficulty. "He will not harm you."

The stranger watched the exchange in cryptic silence, his arms crossed over his chest.

Rowena searched her father's face, blindly hoping for a burst of laughter to explain away the knight's intrusion as a cruel jest. The hope that flickered within her sputtered and died, smothered by the bleakness in the cornflower-blue eyes that were a pale, rheumy echo of her own.

"I shall go with him, Papa, if you say I should."

The man moved forward, unlooping the rope at his waist. Papa stepped back to keep a healthy sword's distance away from the imposing figure.

Rowena shoved her hands behind her back. "There is no need to bind me."

The man retrieved her hands. Rowena did not

flinch as he bound her wrists in front of her none too gently.

Her soft tone belied her anger. "If Papa says I am to go with you, then I will go."

The dark head remained bowed as he tightened the knot with a stiff jerk. Coiling the free end of the rope around his wrist, he led her to the door without a word. She slowed to scoop up her cap. Feeling the sudden tautness in the rope, the man tugged. Rowena dug her heels into the flagstones, resisting his pull. Their eyes met in a silent battle of wills. Without warning, he yanked the rope, causing Rowena to stumble. She straightened, her eyes shining with angry tears for an instant. Then their blue depths cleared and she purposefully followed him through the door, cap clutched in bound hands.

The boys shuffled after them like the undead in a grim processional. Papa meandered behind. Little Freddie was gripped between two of his brothers; a fierce scowl darkened his fair brow.

Night had fallen. A full moon cast its beams through the scant trees, suffusing the muted landscape with the eerie glow of a bogus daylight. Big Freddie gave a low, admiring whistle as a white stallion seemed to rise from the thin shroud of mist that cloaked the ground. The fog entwined itself around the graceful fetlocks. The creature pranced nervously at the sound of approaching footsteps.

Rowena's eyes were drawn to the golden bridle crowning the massive animal. Jewels of every hue encrusted its length. Why would a man of such wealth come all the way to Revelwood to steal a poor man's child? The knight's forbidding shoulders invited no questions as he mounted the horse and slipped Rowena's tether over the leather pommel. The horse's iron-shod hooves twitched. How close could she follow without being pounded to a pulp?

Irwin stepped in front of the horse as if accustomed to placing his bulk in the path of a steed mounted by a fully armed nobleman. The knight leaned back in the saddle with a sigh.

"Kind sir?" Irwin's voice was a mere squeak, so he cleared his throat and tried again. "Kind sir, I hasten to remind you that you are stealing away our only ray of light in a life of darkness. You pluck the single bloom in our garden of grim desolation. I speak for all of us."

Irwin's cousins looked at one another and scratched their heads. Rowena wished faintly that the knight would run him through and end her embarrassment.

"You make an eloquent plea, lad," the knight replied, surprising them all. "Mayhaps you should plead with her father to make his wagers with more care in the future."

From behind Big Freddie, Papa dared to shoot the man a look of pure hatred.

"You will not relent?" asked Irwin.

"I will not."

"Then I pray the burden of chivalry rests heavily on your shoulders. I pray you will honor my sweet cousin with the same consideration you would grant to the rest of the fair and weaker sex."

Rowena itched to box his ears, remembering the uncountable times she had wrestled him to the ground and pinched him until he squealed for mercy.

The stranger again uttered that short, unpleasant laugh. "Do not fear, lad. I will grant her the same consideration that I would grant to any wench as comely as she. Now stand aside or be trampled."

Irwin tripped to the left as the knight kicked the stallion into a trot. Rowena broke into a lope to avoid being jerked off her feet. She dared break her concentration only long enough for one last hungry look at her family. She heard the soft thud of fist pummeling flesh and a familiar cry as Little Freddie tackled Irwin in blind rage and frustration.

Then they were gone. She focused all of her attention on the rocky turf beneath her feet as her world narrowed to the task of putting one foot in front of the other without falling nose first into the drumming hooves.

THE MARRIAGE WAGER

by
Jane Ashford

After watching her husband gamble his life away, Lady Emma Tarrant was determined to prevent another young man from meeting a similar fate. So she challenged the scoundrel who held his debts to another game. After eight years of war, Colin Wareham thought he'd seen it all, but when Lady Emma accosted him, he was suddenly intrigued—and aroused. So he named his stakes: a loss, and he'd forgive the debts. A win, and the lady must give him her heart. . . .

"Will you discard, sir?"

He looked as if he wished to speak, but in the end he simply laid down a card. Focusing on her hand, Emma tried to concentrate all her attention upon it. But she was aware now of his gaze upon her, of his compelling presence on the other side of the table.

She looked up again. He *was* gazing at her, steadily, curiously. But she could find no threat in his eyes. On the contrary, they were disarmingly friendly. He could not possibly look like that and wish her any harm, Emma thought dreamily.

He smiled.

Emma caught her breath. His smile was amazing—warm, confiding, utterly trustworthy. She must have misjudged him, Emma thought.

"Are you sure you won't have some of this excellent brandy?" he asked, sipping from his glass. "I really can recommend it."

Seven years of hard lessons came crashing back upon Emma as their locked gaze broke. He was doing this on purpose, of course. Trying to divert her attention, beguile her into making mistakes and losing. Gathering all her bitterness and resolution, Emma shifted her mind to the cards. She would not be caught so again.

Emma won the second hand, putting them even. But as she exulted in the win, she noticed a small smile playing around Colin Wareham's lips and wondered at it. He poured himself another glass of brandy and sipped it. He looked as if he was thoroughly enjoying himself, she thought. And he didn't seem at all worried that she might beat him. His arrogance was infuriating.

All now rested on the third hand. As she opened a new pack of cards and prepared to deal, Emma took a deep breath.

"You are making a mistake, refusing this brandy," Colin said, sipping again.

"I have no intention of fuzzing my wits with drink," answered Emma crisply. She did not look at him as she snapped out the cards.

"Who are you?" he said abruptly. "Where do you come from? You have the voice and manner of a nobleman's daughter, but you are nothing like the women I meet in society."

Emma flushed a little. There was something in his tone—it might be admiration or derision—that made her self-conscious. Let some of those women spend the last seven years as she had, she thought bitterly, and then see what they were like. "I came here to play cards," she said coldly. "I have said I do not wish to converse with you."

Raising one dark eyebrow, he picked up his hand. The fire hissed in the grate. One of the candles guttered, filling the room with the smell of wax and smoke. At this late hour, the streets outside were silent; the only sounds were Ferik's surprisingly delicate snores from the hall.

In silence, they frowned over discards and calculated odds. Finally, after a long struggle, Wareham said, "I believe this point is good." He put down a card.

Emma stared at it.

"And also my quint," he added, laying down another.

Emma's eyes flickered to his face, then down again.

"Yes?" he urged.

Swallowing, she nodded.

"Ah. Good. Then—a quint, a tierce, fourteen aces, three kings, and eleven cards played, ma'am."

Emma gazed at the galaxy of court cards which he spread before her, then fixed on the one card he still held. The game depended on it, and there was no hint to tell her what she should keep to win the day. She hesitated a moment longer, then made her decision. "A diamond," she said, throwing down the rest of her hand.

"Too bad," he replied, exhibiting a small club.

Emma stared at the square of pasteboard, stunned. She couldn't believe that he had beaten her. "Piqued, repiqued, and capotted," she murmured. It was a humiliating defeat for one with her skill.

"Bad luck."

"I cannot believe you kept that club."

"Rather than throw it away on the slender chance of picking up an ace or a king?"

Numbly, Emma nodded. "You had been taking such risks."

"I sometimes bet on the slim chances," he conceded. "But you must vary your play if you expect to keep your opponent off-balance." He smiled.

That charming smile, Emma thought. Not gloating or contemptuous, but warm all the way to those extraordinary eyes. It almost softened the blow of losing. Almost.

"We said nothing of your stake for this game," he pointed out.

"You asked me for none," Emma retorted. She could not nearly match the amount of Robin Bellingham's notes.

"True." He watched as she bit her lower lip in frustration, and savored the rapid rise and fall of her breasts under the thin bodice of her satin gown. "It appears we are even."

She pounded her fist softly on the table. She had been sure she could beat him, Colin thought. And she had not planned beyond that point. He waited, curious to see what she would do now.

She pounded the table again, thwarted determination obvious in her face. "Will you try another match?" she said finally.

A fighter, Colin thought approvingly. He breathed in the scent of her perfume, let his eyes linger on the creamy skin of her shoulders. He had never encountered such a woman before. He didn't want her to go. On the contrary, he found himself wanting something quite different. "One hand," he offered. "If you win, the notes are yours."

"And if I do not?" she asked.

"You may still have them, but I get . . ." He hesitated. He was not the sort of man who seduced young ladies for sport. But she had come here to his house and challenged him, Colin thought. She was no schoolgirl. She had intrigued and irritated and roused him.

"What?" she said rather loudly.

He had been staring at her far too intensely, Colin realized. But the brandy and the strangeness of the night had made him reckless. "You," he replied.

On sale in November:

AFTER CAROLINE
by Kay Hooper

BREAKFAST IN BED
by Sandra Brown

DON'T TALK TO STRANGERS
by Bethany Campbell

LORD SAVAGE
by Patricia Coughlin

LOVE'S A STAGE
by Sharon and Tom Curtis

DON'T MISS THESE FABULOUS
BANTAM WOMEN'S FICTION TITLES

On Sale in October

From the nationally bestselling TERESA MEDEIROS,
author of *Breath of Magic*, comes a medieval love story
rich with humor and passion.

SHADOWS AND LACE

When Rowena's drunken father gambled her away into the
service of a forbidding knight accused of murder, the Dark Lord
of Caerleon thought he could use her to slay the ghosts of his
past. But soon he would be ensnared by his own trap—slave to
a desire he could never hope to quench. ____ 57623-2 $5.99/$7.99

THE MARRIAGE WAGER

by JANE ASHFORD

"An exceptional talent with a tremendous gift for involving
her readers in the story." —*Rendezvous*

Determined to prevent another young man from gambling away
his life, Lady Emma Tarrant challenged the scoundrel who held
his debts to a game of chance. Intrigued, Lord Colin Wareham
named his stakes: a loss, and he'd forgive the debts. A win, and
the lady must give him her heart. ____ 57577-5 $5.99/$7.99

"An emotionally poignant historical romance
that will thrill readers of the genre, particularly fans
of Julie Garwood." —*Affaire de Coeur*

Ask for these books at your local bookstore or use this page to order.

Please send me the books I have checked above. I am enclosing $____ (add $2.50 to
cover postage and handling). Send check or money order, no cash or C.O.D.'s, please.

Name _____

Address _____

City/State/Zip _____

Send order to: Bantam Books, Dept. FN158, 2451 S. Wolf Rd., Des Plaines, IL 60018.
Allow four to six weeks for delivery.

Prices and availability subject to change without notice. FN 158 10/96